Raves for: GO AND COME BACK

★"Abelove's remarkable gift is letting readers see their own culture through the eyes of someone whose values are completely different. . . . Full of life and packed with characters that by turns irritate and enlighten, *Go and Come Back* is a startling, vibrant read." —*Booklist,* starred review

★"Compelling. . . . The spirited heroine evokes Karen Cushman's [Newbery Honor Book] *Catherine, Called Birdy*." —*SLJ,* starred review

"*Go and Come Back* is a beautiful novel . . . understated, delicate, and yet powerful. I recommend it as providing an intimate portrait of a different but very human way of life." —Thomas Gregor, Professor of Anthropology, Vanderbilt University

>─┼─◇─○─◇─┼─◄

A *Publishers Weekly* Best Book of the Year
An *SLJ* Best Book of the Year
A *Horn Book* Fanfare Book

OTHER PUFFIN BOOKS YOU MAY ENJOY

GO AND COME BACK

JOAN ABELOVE

PUFFIN BOOKS

PUFFIN BOOKS
Published by the Penguin Group
Penguin Putnam Books for Young Readers,
345 Hudson Street, New York, New York 10014, U.S.A.
Penguin Books Ltd, 27 Wrights Lane, London W8 5TZ, England
Penguin Books Australia Ltd, Ringwood, Victoria, Australia
Penguin Books Canada Ltd, 10 Alcorn Avenue, Toronto, Ontario, Canada M4V 3B2
Penguin Books (N.Z.) Ltd, 182-190 Wairau Road, Auckland 10, New Zealand

Penguin Books Ltd, Registered Offices: Harmondsworth, Middlesex, England

First published in the United States of America by DK Publishing, Inc., 1998
Published by Puffin Books,
a division of Penguin Putnam Books for Young Readers, 2000

9 10 8

LIBRARY OF CONGRESS CATALOGING-IN-PUBLICATION DATA
Abelove, Joan.
Go and come back / Joan Abelove.
p. cm.
Summary: Alicia, a young tribeswoman living in a village in the Amazonian jungle of Peru, tells
about the two American women anthropologists who arrive to study her people's way of life.
[1. Anthropologists—Fiction. 2. Amazon River Valley—Fiction. 3. Peru—Fiction.] I. Title.
PZ7.A1594 Go 2000 [Fic]—dc21 99-054230
ISBN 0-14-130694-7

Printed in the United States of America

Cover based on original photographs by
Joan Abelove and Roberta Campos.
Adapted by Lori Thorn.

For the villagers of "Poincushmana"
and most of all,
for Guillermina and Roberta,
and Steve, and Andy.

This book is based on events that took place during the early 1970s. The "two old white ladies" were actually in their late twenties. The Isabos live in the Amazonian jungle of Peru, along the eastern slopes of the Andes, much as their ancestors have for centuries.

GO AND
COME BACK

CHAPTER ONE Two old white ladies came to our village late one day, just before dinnertime, at the beginning of the dry season. Everyone else ran down the riverbank to greet them. I stood at the top. I could see them fine from up there. I had better things to do than run to greet old white ladies.

It was Nonti, my mother's brother's wife's brother, who had brought them up the river. When he docked, the two women stayed in the boat. They sat and smiled. Every so often they would talk to each other in some language none of us could understand. And then they would smile some more. Only their mouths moved. The other parts of their bodies were as still as when there is no wind at all, just before a big rain comes.

Nonti told us they were called anthropologists. They

looked like plain old gringos to me. One was very tall and skinny, with long yellow hair. The other one looked a little more like us, nice and fat and not tall, but her skin was a funny shade of pink. Her hair was not black enough or straight enough. It was long, but she had no bangs. They both wore no beads, no nose rings, no lip plugs, no anklets. They didn't pierce their noses or their lower lips. They didn't bind their ankles or flatten their foreheads. They did nothing to make themselves beautiful.

Elena, my mother's sister's daughter, hopped right into the boat where the two women were sitting. She pointed to the tall one's head and said, "Mapeu!" Head. They looked at each other and repeated, "Mapeu." But they said it more like "mopu." Elena clapped. "Look at them! This big tall one has hair like thatch. Can you believe it? We could cut her hair off and patch the hole in our roof!"

Everyone laughed. Even me. Elena always makes me laugh. And then the white women laughed too. But they didn't know what was funny.

"Elena, how could you jump into their boat?" I asked her when she hopped out and came back up the bank to me. "And point at their heads and talk to them? How could you do it? I wouldn't get that close to them."

"Oh, Alicia. You're such a worrier. What harm could it do?"

"*You* worry about nothing! Like a child!"

"You should have more fun, Alicia. That old man husband of yours will come back soon enough. Then will be the time to be worried and unhappy."

"He's not my husband. My father was drunk when he promised me. I have no husband. My father was drunk!" I hated it when anyone said I had a husband. I didn't have one. "And *your* old husband only brings home tiny birds when he goes out hunting," I told her. "Soon you won't be so nice and fat, if you have to eat only what he brings home."

Elena laughed and stuck her tongue out at me. Elena would always be fat. Not like me—skinny, ugly me. I would never get fat. No matter how much I ate, how tight I tied my honshe, my ankle bands, how much fat medicine my mother gave me. "Skinny Alicia. Your legs look like two cotton threads hanging from your skirt." Ugly.

Elena was beautiful—short, fat, with round cheeks and a big hearty laugh. Elena laughed at everything and everybody. She made fun of people and things all the time. She did it so they would like her. It usually worked. Me, I was not so sociable.

3

The old ladies sat in Nonti's boat and smiled. What did they want from us?

"Do they speak anything anyone can understand?" asked Angel, our schoolteacher. Everyone laughed.

"Nawa, all nawa are the same," muttered old man Chichica. "They all eat snakes and have sex with dogs."

"They speak Spanish and something else. They came from the New York City," Nonti was saying. "And I have taken them on a trip up and down your Paro River, looking for a village to live in. They want to live here, in Poincushmana."

Live here, with us! Why would they do such a thing?

The old ladies sat and smiled.

Everyone started asking questions at once.

"Did they bring any liquor with them?"

"Did they bring pictures of their Jesus?" Swiss missionaries had brought us funny pictures of their god carrying a big, oddly formed piece of firewood, dragging it on his back up a steep hill.

"Have they come to steal our children?"

"Have they come to steal the fat from our bodies?"

"Will they kill us all while we sleep?"

Old man Ashandi roared with laughter. "They don't look like they could even take care of themselves, let alone steal our children or our lives. Look at the tall

4

one—she is so scrawny. You can practically see through her skin, it is so pale."

"They look weak, but they're not," Nonti said. "They ask many stupid questions. But they are not mean. They are just incredibly ignorant."

"They will stay at my house," Papaisi, the headman, announced, and told his daughters to go prepare dinner for the visitors.

The old ladies stayed in the boat, still sitting, still not moving. They just sat and smiled.

What were these old women doing here, so far away from their homes, from their parents, far from husbands and children? What could make women travel so far all by themselves? It wasn't until later that we learned the most shocking part—these two women weren't even related to each other. Not in any way. They were what they call friends, amigos in Spanish, no word in Isabo. So they were really alone. One stranger and another stranger. Two strangers. All alone.

CHAPTER TWO Nonti was fussing with his motor. He pointed at me, squatting at the top of the bank. "You, Alicia, my sister's husband's sister's daughter. Take them on a walk through the village. They like to do that." Nonti tapped the old ladies and pointed to me, telling them that I would be their guide.

Why me? I hadn't jumped into their boat. And I wasn't a child to be ordered around. My blood had come three times already. Why did they want to walk through the village? What did that mean? They had been sitting so long in the boat, I didn't know if their legs worked. I wasn't going to carry them up the riverbank!

My little brother Marco ran up to the old ladies, grabbed the short one by her hand, and started pulling her out of the boat and up the riverbank. "Come on," he said in his schoolboy Spanish. "*I'll* show you our village. Do you play the guitar? Angel has an old guitar."

Marco pretended to play a guitar until the old ladies looked like they understood.

"Guitarra," the big one said. She pointed to the short one, who nodded and nodded and pretended to strum a guitar just like Marco. "Joanna," she told him. "And I am Margarita."

"We'll take you to Angel's house," said Marco. "You can play for us. Come on."

Everyone was braver than me—Elena and now my younger brother.

The old ladies followed Marco up the hill. They had arrived when the river was low, so the riverbank was steep, so steep that you could only see the tops of the houses from the river. The old ladies bent over and climbed the dusty bank. They used their hands like feet, digging their hand heels into the dirt to steady themselves.

"They walk like monkeys," I said to Marco.

He nodded. "Like clumsy monkeys," he said.

When they got to the top, the old ladies stood up and dusted the dirt off their hands. Marco stretched his arm out.

"Here is our home," he said. "Here on this side are

the kitchens where the mothers of our families work to prepare food for us, so that we can grow strong and bring back much meat." He pointed to the kitchens lined up next to the river, like the kernels on an ear of corn.

"Marco, you sound like a pompous old man," I whispered to him.

"Shut up," he said. "I am their guide. I will tell them how we live."

"Stupid," I muttered, and Marco continued with his speech.

He was not telling about our real lives, about how we really live. Marco was gesturing to all the houses in Poincushmana as if we were all the same, as if my mother's neat house was the same as Elena's mother's house, where their clothes were thrown all over the floor, never hung over the rafters neatly; as if every mother cooked the same way; as if every man was a good hunter; as if every mother treated her children the same.

I looked up and down the village. Our village must look beautiful from the sky, the way the missionaries see it when they fly in. From the sky you could see the straight line of houses on the forest side, the straight line of kitchens on the river side, and the wide path that separates the houses from the kitchens. Four straight lines—river, kitchens, path, and houses. Like a design woven into cloth.

Marco led the old ladies to the path that separates the line of kitchens from the line of houses.

As we were walking, my mother's sisters' children came to join us, chattering about these old women, touching them, smelling them, and laughing.

"Why do they wear pants?"

"Are they women with penises?"

"What funny hair they have. It smells like caimito fruit."

"Look, the short one has a ring that looks like a silver fish."

I looked at the short one's hand. The ring was beautiful, a shiny silver fish wrapped around her finger.

"Feel their hands! Their skin is so soft, like cotton."

"How long that tall one's neck is."

"Her skin is so white it has blue lines in it, like the salt from the mountains."

"Let's run!"

We had arrived at the pasto, the space that separated my mother's house from the house where Angel, the teacher, lived. This pasto was overgrown. A narrow path was worn through the middle; the grass was knee-high on either side. Running through the pasto would scare away any snakes hidden in the weeds. We all ran, my brother and I and Elena and all my mother's sisters' children, pulling the old ladies along. They seemed to like running. We got to the other side, laughing. The old ladies were out of breath but happy. Their smiles were different now. They were happy smiles, not stiff ones like they had worn in Nonti's boat.

It was getting late by the time Angel gave this Joanna his guitar. We all sat down in the cleared space outside of Angel's house with the children from Angel's house, Angel, and his two wives. The mosquitoes were starting to appear, and we all swatted at them. Joanna turned the knobs on the guitar and made some sounds.

"I don't like their music," Marco said to me.

"I don't think she started playing yet," I told him. "The Swiss missionary used to do the same thing. It takes them awhile to start."

Soon Joanna began to use her fingers differently, and the sounds from the guitar were loud and rhythmic, not like anything we had heard before, louder and deeper than the missionary's. And then Joanna sang. She sang about my favorite kind of bananas. Shboom.

We all laughed. "Shboom, shboom," Joanna sang.

"Sing the banana song again," Marco said when she ended.

11

Joanna said the song was in her language, that shboom was a word in the English. The tall one, Margarita, agreed.

"But what does shboom *mean* in your language?" Angel asked them. As if it could mean anything but the sweet tiny bananas that ripen in the wet season.

"It means nothing," the tall one explained. "Just a nice sound to sing."

How strange to sing big, loud, long songs about nothing, about a made-up word, sounds that mean nothing, like the way babies talk. These were grown-up women, singing like babies.

"Nothing but big old babies," my mother said when I got home. "Big old babies with no sense."

She was right. Big old strange-looking babies. "But I like their music," I said.

"Baby music," my mother muttered. "My daughter likes nawa baby music."

CHAPTER THREE Papaisi, the headman, blew the horn to call a meeting of the whole village that night to find out what these old ladies wanted from us. Everyone came and sat outside Papaisi's house, on the path between his house and his kitchen. The moon was full, and, along with the stars, it lit the path. We sat swatting mosquitoes, making jokes about these white women. We could say anything we wanted. The old ladies didn't understand a word.

"They want to live in our village for one year, from this dry season to the end of the next dry season," Papaisi said. "That is why they have come, to ask if they can live with us. The tall one, Margarita, wants to learn about agriculture. The fat one, Joanna, will study babies."

Everyone talked at once.

"Where are their husbands?"

"Where are their children?"

"Will they bring us sugarcane liquor?"

"They will not bring us anything. Just like the missionaries."

"Let the old ladies stay," Elena said. "You can ask them all these questions."

I kept my eyes on the old ladies. The tall one had blue eyes! Rambi!

The headman asked them in Spanish what they would do with everything they learned from us.

"We will write books," said Margarita, the big one.

"Will your book be big?" Papaisi asked.

"Yes. And there will be two books. We will each write a book."

Elena came and sat next to me.

"What could they write about us that would fill up two books?" I whispered to her. "What is there to study about babies and agriculture?" Babies are healthy, they are sick, they eat, they cry, they pee, they poop, they live, they die. Agriculture is the same as babies. The plantains and yuca grow, or they die. What is there to study?

"So?" Elena said. "It will be interesting to have them

live with us. They will be fun to watch. And they will bring us things."

"I don't think so," I said. "They look very stingy to me." Yohuashi. They both wore gold earrings, gold watches, and good sturdy shoes. They must be rich. But they had given us nothing. Not a cracker, not a piece of candy, not a stick of gum. Nothing.

"Everyone looks stingy to you," Elena said. "They won't be. They will be different. It will be good."

"Everyone looks good to you," I said. "Remember when I saw the missionaries that way? The ones who said whoever believed could have their tape recorders with their songs that I liked?"

"Yes," said Elena. "I remember them. You became a believer because you liked their music."

"Yes. I believed. And then the tape recorder broke!"

"And you stopped believing."

"Yes," I said. "And they took the broken tape recorder away and never came back."

"What harm was there?" Elena asked. "You got to listen to the songs for a while."

Papaisi spoke in a loud voice. "The village says that you can live with us."

The old ladies smiled and said that in exchange for letting them live here, they would bring us medicine.

15

Papaisi, not to be outdone by old white women, announced in his most important voice, "And we will build you a house."

"They will bring us medicine," my mother mumbled, "but will they give us any?"

The next morning, all the men in the village started digging the postholes for the old ladies' house, right next to Papaisi's. Our houses are beautiful, four big perfectly straight posts, a thatched roof, and a floor, open on all sides to the breezes. We have no furniture to clutter up the house, just nice soft floor wood to lie on or sit on, our sleeping mats, our mosquito nets slung over the rafters, and our clothes, also slung over the rafters or on the floor, to use to rest your head on something soft.

The old ladies kept saying they would be happy to move into any old house we had, any house no one was using. Whoever heard of a house no one was using? Were they fools? Nawa! An old house? An unused house? It takes a long time and a lot of people to build a house. Why would we have one that we didn't use? Build a house and let it go to waste? Is that what they did in the New York? Spend months building something just to leave it alone? Maybe they did have sex with dogs! We are not nawa, I thought. We build houses to live in, not to let them rot and fall down.

The old ladies were happy. They got out their cameras and took pictures of the men digging the postholes. They smiled and smiled and told us they would be back soon, they had to go to Pucallpa and get their supplies, whatever that would be. Then they got into Nonti's boat and started down the river. Everyone stopped working on the house. Who knew if they were really coming back? We don't build houses for the fun of it.

That afternoon Elena came by with her gathering basket.

"Let's go gathering," she said. "Come, the caimito are ripe upriver."

I put down my embroidery.

"Good," I said. "I hate this skirt. My stitches are so messy."

I took my gathering basket and we started walking upriver, reboqui.

"Who are you meeting?" I asked Elena.

Going gathering sometimes means that you are going to meet one of your boyfriends. Elena had many. Fat, beautiful, bold Elena. I had only one, Boshi, and he was in Tarapoto working with his father.

"No one," she said.

17

"Elena, I will see when we get there, you stingy one. Tell me now, ishton!"

"No, really. I just wanted to go gathering. I have the taste for caimito."

We made our way along a path behind the houses that led upriver to a good caimito grove. Elena was moving slowly, her feet dragging through the dry dirt.

"What's wrong?" I asked.

"Later, when we are farther away from the village," Elena whispered.

When we got to where the caimitos were, Elena threw her basket down on the ground and sat.

I squatted next to her, picked up a twig, and began drawing in the dirt.

"Era toya riqui," Elena said. I am pregnant.

Toya. Elena would be the first one my age to be a mother. "What about the plant you were taking, the one you found in the monte, the one that was supposed to make you not get pregnant?"

"The plant died," said Elena.

"Oh," I said.

"Alicia, I don't want to have a baby. I don't want to be a mother. I have not been a child long enough. And I am scared. Scared I will die, scared I will die giving birth."

18

"I know," I said. "I know."

Elena and I had been little girls together, we had played at being mothers together, we had been in school together. And now we were beginning the end of our lives together, beginning the time of being wives, of being mothers, the last part of our lives.

Elena began to cry. "I don't want this. I don't want this. I want to go back to the time when we were little, so I could grow up again, so I would not be getting old, so I would not be so close to death."

Elena had worried about dying ever since we were little. I worried too, but it was different with Elena. Stronger. Coshi biris.

"Maybe it's not true, maybe you are not pregnant," I said.

"Maybe," Elena said, wiping her eyes. "And maybe not. Whatever it would be."

"Whatever it would be," I repeated. We sat quietly.

"Elena," I said, "let's play, like we did when we were little. Let's play right now, right here. Let's play again."

Elena laughed. "You are so funny, so tsindi," she said. "I am going to be a mother, and you want me to play."

"Yes," I said, "yes. Let's do it now, before we forget,

before we don't know how, before we don't want to anymore."

I sprang up and started to collect small branches and twigs. "Come on," I said. "Let's build a campamento. Remember?"

"Yes," said Elena. "Of course I remember."

We gathered twigs and branches and made little sleeping places and a hearth and pretended we were cooking bananas and yuca while our husbands went out to the monte hunting for meat.

"Careful your fire doesn't get too big," Elena yelled at me. She used a deep voice, the voice she used to use back then to sound like a woman. "You are so messy you will set the whole forest on fire."

Elena always said that when we were little, even though we never had real fires to play with.

"And your fire is so neat and tiny that nothing will ever get cooked on it," I said in my child voice. "Now let's pretend that we are at a party and we get drunk and we sing our old women songs.

"Nocon hande Metza Alicia," I sang.

My name is Beautiful Alicia. Hear my song. Listen to my song, for I sing it for you, to remember and to tell the others, to tell forever, to sing my song forever. My name is Beautiful Alicia.

I wondered if all old women thought of themselves as beautiful, or did they sing these songs to make the spirits think they were?

"Nocon hande Metza Elena," Elena sang with me. We sang standing together, our arms around each other's shoulders, swaying like old women sway when they sing their old women songs.

Then we gathered some of the ripe caimitos and walked back to the village.

Before we got there, I whispered to Elena, "Min himbi bishonhue." May your blood come.

Elena smiled. "Nocon himbi bishon raibirai." May it come or whatever.

CHAPTER FOUR   Life went on. The gnats came out in the morning, the mosquitoes when the sun set. Some good things happened, some bad. Cornelia's baby was born. Philiberto's baby died. Metza Shoko cured Amalia's stomachache. Yamiquenti still didn't get pregnant. Elena's younger brother Nelson had sex for the first time. Potonko adopted Lucia's daughter. Boshi brought me yellow and red thread from Tarapoto and went off to work wood upriver with Jose Elenario. And Elena's blood came. That was very good. Hacon shama himbi. The old man I was promised to stayed where he was— two days downriver working at his patrón's farm with his first wife, my older sister Maya, and their two children. That was good too. The postholes for the old ladies' house remained the same as when the two old ladies went off downriver. We didn't expect them to come back.

A week after the old ladies left, a Peruvian regatón, a trader called Paco, docked his boat in front of my house. Paco's wife, Carmella, and their new baby were with him. The men went down to see how much sugarcane liquor he had for sale. He had a lot and Angel bought a lot. A party, we all thought. And it was. But in the middle of the night, after everyone was asleep, I heard screaming and weeping down by the river. I sneaked down and saw Carmella, the trader's wife, sobbing on the shore, holding a bundle in her arms. She was alone and crying so hard she shook all over. The boat was gone.

"What's wrong?" I asked her softly in Spanish. I had learned to speak some Spanish in school, but I was better at understanding than speaking it.

"My idiot of a husband has decided that this baby is not his. He says he is going to throw her in the river when he returns. My baby, his own daughter, and he will throw her in the river. What am I going to do?" She sobbed and rocked the baby.

How could her stupid old drunken husband think of killing this little bundle? "I'll take the baby for you," I blurted out. "I have no children yet. I could care for her." I could. I would. The baby was a girl! Whoever heard of killing a girl baby?

"You would?" she asked, looking up at me for the first time.

"Yes," I said. "I'll ask the other mothers in the village to nurse her. At least she'll be alive."

It wasn't like becoming a mother, although I was old enough for that. This was different. This was saving the baby's life. It was me saving the baby. Just me. I was not becoming a mother, I was not becoming a wife. I was making sure that this little bundle did not die. At least that she did not die tonight, at the hands of her father.

We both heard the sound of Paco's boat returning from upriver, reboqui.

"Take her," Carmella said. "He's drunk enough to come back and throw her in the river now." She patted the bundle gently, handed it to me, and ran to meet her husband's boat.

It was too dark to see the baby well, but she didn't weigh much. She was light in my arms and sound asleep. I went back to my house before Paco returned. From my kitchen, I heard the boat stop and then go again, this time downriver. Paco and his wife were gone, and I had a new baby. A nawa baby.

"Well, little one," I whispered. "It's just you and me now. No one else is going to like you. They will all think I am crazy, trying to save a little nawa runt. But we'll be all right, you and me. My father is downriver hunting. He will be back tomorrow or the next day, and then we will have lots of meat to eat. Good night now, little one."

Everybody was too drunk that night to notice anything. And this baby didn't cry at all. Amazing. In the morning, I got up first and stirred the hearth to heat some chapo to feed her. My mother stumbled out of her mosquito net and saw me sitting with the baby at the fire.

"Whose little one have you got there?" she asked me.

"She used to be Carmella's, but she's mine now," I said, and told her the whole story.

"Why did you take a nawa baby, you silly thing? Even if she is a girl, she is still a nawa." She opened the blanket I had her wrapped in and took a good look.

"She won't live long," she said. "She's too scrawny —like a sickly chicken. Here, give her to me. I'll give her some of your little brother's food." She put the baby to her breast. "That old nawa was going to kill her? Kill a girl baby. Nawa! They have no sense at all."

She was right. No one kills a girl baby. Girls are the

ones who stay home and make sure your old age is happy and easy. Boys go off and never take care of you. You might kill a boy baby, if he were deformed or you didn't want another child. But no Isabo had ever killed a girl child.

"It doesn't matter," my mother went on. "She won't live long enough to grow up."

I wasn't sure she would either. But if she didn't, it wasn't going to be because I didn't try. I was going to save this little nawa baby. I had to do it. My mother's sister, Nachi, would understand. She was raising Resho because Resho's mother didn't want her. Resho's father was a Peruvian, a nawa. When Resho was born, Nachi said, "I will raise her." Now Nachi was Resho's mother, her tita, her onan tita, her adoptive mother. Nachi would understand.

Later that morning, Elena came over with her gathering basket and sat down next to me. My mother was in her garden.

"Let me see the baby," she said.

"She's asleep in my brother's hammock," I said. Elena peeked inside the hammock.

"She is so skinny," she said. "She won't live long."

"Live or whatever," I said.

"Does your mother feed her?"

27

"Yes. And I make her some sweet banana chapo and let her suck it from my finger."

"Was Carmella really going to kill her?"

"No, Paco wanted to kill her. Carmella wanted to save her."

"Nawa," she said, and spit on the ground. "Where were Carmella's kinswomen? Why didn't they take this baby?"

"I don't know. Wherever they would be. Carmella was sure Paco would kill the baby. She was sure of that."

"Nawa," Elena said again. "They are worse than animals." She leaned over the baby's hammock. "You are a lucky little one. Alicia will keep you alive. If anyone can keep you alive, it is Alicia." She smiled at me. "Coshi biris ainbo." You are a strong girl.

"Coshi raibirai," I said. Strong or whatever.

CHAPTER FIVE My father came home from his hunting trip that afternoon with a lot of meat—a deer, a white-lipped peccary, an armadillo, and a few small birds. He stayed for a few days and then went to work downriver for Juan Matus. The following morning Marco stopped in the middle of the path between our house and our kitchen, cocked his head, and yelled, "They're coming back! They're coming back!"

My mother was horrified. She dropped the pot she was stirring in the kitchen and ran into the house, carrying my baby brother on her hip.

"Yoshin, yoshin, canoncahue," my mother screamed at us all. "Get into the house, all of you. Spirits are coming!"

Marco fell on the ground laughing. My mother was

furious. "Spirits are not to be laughed at, you ignorant child!"

Marco could not stop laughing. By the time my mother got to him and began pulling him into the house, tears were streaming down his face and he was limp from laughing. I think my mother was about to slap him when he finally managed to say, "Not spirits, Mama. Not spirits. The white ladies. I heard Nonti's pequi-pequi. About three days away."

Marco had sharp ears—like a jaguar. No one else had heard Nonti's pequi-pequi. The rest of us heard it a day later, after the boat had turned the two big vueltas just below Moshi. Everyone can hear a boat when it's two days downriver. The Paro is like a coiled snake, so that when a boat is at Moshi, two days away by river, it is very close by sound.

Papaisi told Chawa, his youngest daughter, that the white ladies would stay with her until their house was built. Chawa was delighted. She is the youngest of three wives and is always whining, begging for things—["I am so poor, I have nothing, I am the youngest wife of three and my husband gives me nothing."] Now she thought she would have all the old ladies' things to herself.

The next afternoon I was sitting in my house, embroidering a skirt. My nawa was asleep in an old hammock my mother had strung up.

"Hohue," my mother's sister Nachi said, and sat down next to me.

"Hoho," I responded. "Hainqui mia itai?" Are you here?

"Hain ea itai," she said. I am here.

Nachi looked at the skirt I was making.

"Nice," she said. "Your embroidery is much better. You are growing up."

We sat for a while, Nachi watching me stitch.

"Min nawa oshai?" she finally asked. Is your nawa asleep?

"Oshai. Oinhue." She's asleep. Go look at her.

Nachi pulled back the hammock and peeked inside.

"She's very tiny, very skinny. But beautiful, for a nawa. Like Resho, but paler. Resho was scrawny like this one. But not as pale. Maybe she will get some color as she grows." Nachi kept looking at my sleeping baby. The baby stirred, and Nachi swung her hammock very gently.

"Everyone says you are crazy to take this baby. You are too young, you will soon have your own children,

you have no good reason to try and save this child."
Nachi stopped talking then and just looked at the baby.

"What do you call her?" she asked.

"I call her my nawa," I said.

"You should name her," said Nachi. "She will be
more likely to live if you name her."

I nodded. She was right. A child with no name had
no chance to live, especially when the child had so little
chance anyway.

"Metza Cami. I will call her Metza Cami," I said.
Metza means pretty, and Cami is my favorite fruit. It
also sounded like her mother's name, Carmella.

"Metza Cami," said Nachi. "Nice. A good name. A
good name for a beautiful baby. She is beautiful, you
know. Sometimes it's hard to tell, but look at her. She
will have good hair, it is dark and straight, and her eyebrows are lovely. See what a nice shape they have?"
Nachi passed her finger lightly over Cami's tiny eyebrows. Cami twitched her nose and then was still.

"Her mother already pierced her ears. Now you must
do the rest."

"The rest?" I asked.

"She is your daughter now. You must treat her right.
You must flatten her forehead, pierce her nose and her
lip."

"But she is a nawa," I said. "I just saved her from being killed."

"She is your daughter now," Nachi repeated. "You are her mother. You must treat her well. Make her beautiful. Here, I brought you Resho's old wintoti."

I am not her mother, I thought. I saved her from dying, that's all.

Nachi reached into her blouse and gave me the forehead flattening board she had used on Resho. The cloth covering was old and faded and the ties were frayed. The cotton stuffing that protects the head from the wood was coming out. Nachi stuffed the cotton back under the cloth and put the wintoti on Cami's forehead, carefully tying it around the back of her head. Cami slept.

"Only keep it on her in the morning," she said. "That is enough time each day. We will wait to pierce her lip and nose. She needs to eat better. She might stop eating if her nose and lip are sore. We will do that later, when she is fat."

CHAPTER SIX   Nonti's boat arrived three days later, at dinnertime. Not that there was much dinner that night. A lot of the men were off on hunting trips, so there was very little meat anywhere. We all ran down to the shore when they docked. Maybe they had brought some meat.

They hadn't, although they had brought everything else in the world. Nonti's entire boat was filled with their stuff, boxes and boxes. We had no idea what it all was. We would have to wait and watch them unpack. But first they must have brought sugarcane liquor for a party. Surely they did that. Nonti would know to tell them to be sure and bring lots of liquor to have a party to welcome them.

We all helped carry their things up the bank and put

them in Chawa's house. I carried a big box. I tried to shake it while I carried it up the bank, but it made no sound. It was heavy, packed solid. With what? I couldn't guess. The old ladies looked surprised not to have their own house yet, but Chawa, the shoya, the rat, kept smiling and ushering them into her house and telling them there was plenty of room for them and all their stuff. Plenty of room. Chawa kept carrying boxes up the bank to her house, piling them on her floor, smiling from ear to ear.

And there was a big plastic jug of sugarcane liquor. An enormous bottle. Good old Nonti never forgot his kinsmen. Everyone grinned when they saw Chawa's littlest daughter carry that big bottle out of the boat and stagger up to Chawa's house. So there was no meat today or yesterday and none coming in tomorrow. At least we could have a fiesta tonight! And maybe they would give me some rice and sugar to feed my nawa baby, my Cami.

But nothing was simple with these old ladies. They brought in a big bottle of sugarcane liquor, enough to keep the whole village drunk for a day and a half, and they didn't want to open the bottle. They were saving it. What was the matter with them? Did they think it would get better with age? When you have liquor, you drink it. When you have food, you eat it. It's only natural. When you have food, you make sure to be generous and give some to all your relatives, so when they have some, they will share it with you. That is how you "save" food. The same with liquor. Where did these people come from? How did they live with such stupid ideas? I was upset. We were all upset. The whole village. Nonti tried to talk to the old ladies.

"I see the village as very sad," he began.

"Sad?" asked Joanna. "What do you mean?"

"They are all sad. Very sad. They want to have a party to welcome you to your new home and now they cannot do so. Therefore, I see that they are very sad." Nonti was careful not to use the word for house, since we had not finished building them their house. He gazed down at the ground and sighed.

The old ladies looked around at everyone. Then they jabbered at each other in their own language. The tall one was really mad. Joanna kept turning the fish ring on her hand. Nonti looked up at them sadly. Then he looked at the village and sighed again. Finally, they told him yes, they would have a party, but they wanted to save half of the sugarcane liquor for a party when their house was finished. They would only have half a party.

Well, that was better than no party. "Now I see the village is happy again," said Nonti.

So we had our party. Angel got out his old record player and went over to the two old ladies to borrow batteries for it. Nonti explained to them that you had to have music for a party, and that the only way to have music was to use their batteries.

"We don't have that many batteries," Joanna said to Nonti. "We need them for our tape recorder, for our work. We can't get any more until our first break, in about eight weeks. Sorry. We can't loan our batteries. We'll just sing at the party."

Poor Nonti. It was his job to try and explain to these two how it was here. They were very bad at understanding.

"It's really not a party without music. Even in your country, people don't have parties without music, do they?" Nonti was trying hard. "The village wants to welcome you with music."

"In our country," said Margarita, holding her head high at the top of her enormously long neck, "if people don't have batteries, they don't play music." And she marched off into the jungle.

Nonti tried again with Joanna. "Surely you can understand. They just want to have a proper party to welcome their new guests into their village. They want to make you happy, to have you dance and sing and be happy." Nonti looked prepared to go on and on until Joanna gave in.

"Okay, okay. How many do you need?"

"Only six," said Angel. "And we won't use them all up. A few songs, a few dances. To welcome you."

"Fine," said Joanna. Maybe she was the one with sense, the one with some kindness. Margarita had just stomped off in anger. Maybe Joanna was not as stingy, not as yohuashi as her friend. Joanna walked into their side of Chawa's house and opened up a big metal box that was *full* of batteries. An entire metal box full of batteries, and they wouldn't even lend us six without putting up a fuss. If she was not as stingy as Margarita, it wasn't by much.

"Make sure and return them," said Joanna. "We need them—"

"For your work," Angel finished her sentence. "Of course. They'll be back before the dawn."

Then he added, in Isabo, "Do you believe how stingy these women are? Maybe that's why they have no children."

None of us laughed. We didn't want Joanna to change her mind and take the batteries back. But we all agreed.

I wondered if maybe they would learn something about how to treat people by living with us. Maybe not.

∽

It was a halfhearted party, since there was only half-hearted liquor. The women didn't put on their best necklaces. The old men didn't wear their best beadwork. My mother didn't even go. "You go," she said to me. "I'll watch your little runt for you. I don't want to go to such a stingy party anyway."

"Cami," I said. "Her name is Cami."

"Whatever it would be." My mother shrugged.

Very soon all the liquor was gone. There had been only enough for the old people. Not enough for us to drink any. Elena and I sat on Chawa's porch, watching.

"Stingy old ladies," I said to Elena. "I was right. See! There is nothing for us to drink."

Elena laughed. "But they are so much fun to watch," she said. "Look at the fat one. Her face is all red. Her poinke is jiggling, and still she just smiles."

The headman was dancing with Joanna, bouncing her up and down with his strong arms as he twirled her around and around.

"I have seven daughters and only one son," the old man announced.

"I am sorry," said Joanna.

He looked at her to see if she was kidding. She seemed serious.

"These women," he said in a loud voice in Isabo. "They don't understand anything."

The old man had been bragging, of course. He had seven daughters and only one son—a powerful man, a man to be reckoned with, [a man who had seven sons-in-law to work for him and only one child he had to give away to work for someone else.] And Joanna had said she was sorry!

"Stingy and stupid," I said to Elena.

"Stingy, stupid, and fun to watch," Elena answered.

Margarita spent a lot of time talking to Nonti at the party. She asked him what they should pay for meat, what a kilo of their rice should be traded for, how to deal with people who kept asking for things, on and on. And she wrote all his answers down in a little orange notebook. She wasn't enjoying the party. She was scared to be alone with us, without Nonti. Joanna just kept dancing with everyone, dancing and smiling. Maybe *she* wasn't scared. Or maybe she was drunk. They saved enough liquor for themselves.

A few old men went to Nonti. "We are too old to

dance," they said. "We want to sing. We need more liquor. We need to be drunker to sing our old men songs. Don't they want to hear our old men songs?"

Nonti translated the old men's requests to the two old ladies. But of course they said no. They were saving the liquor to have a party when their house was finished. Hahuetian raibirai. Whenever that would be.

Old man Chichica was angry. When everyone else was heading for home, I noticed him sneaking around behind Chawa's house where the old ladies had put the rest of the sugarcane liquor. He pulled the bottle off the ledge where they had hidden it, lay down on the ground, and drank the whole thing. Then he passed out, still holding the bottle in his arms, mumbling about stingy old ladies who didn't want anyone to be happy. I knew the old ladies would be furious if they found the old man like that, so I took the bottle out of his hands, went to the river and filled it halfway up, and put it back on the ledge where they had left it. It would be awhile before they were ready to share more liquor with us. And they would never know who had replaced the liquor with river water.

The next morning, Papaisi blew the horn and all the men went to work on the old ladies' house. The old ladies sat with Nonti in Chawa's house. They hired my mother's sister's daughter, Cuncha, to be their cook when their house was finished. Nonti figured out how much they should pay her. Margarita wrote it down. They hired Elena to teach them Isabo. She had been teaching them words ever since she hopped into their boat the day they arrived. Nonti figured out how much they should pay her. Margarita wrote it down. They spent every evening talking to Nonti and writing down what he told them. Then it was time for Nonti to leave.

Shori, the shaman, and old man Ashandi tried to convince the old ladies to have a good-bye party for Nonti. But they said no. The liquor was for the party for their new house. They were saving river water, I thought. Serves them right.

The old ladies actually cried as they watched Nonti's pequi-pequi go downstream.

"Why are they crying?" my mother muttered. "We are not holding them as prisoners. They asked to stay here."

"Now they have to deal with us on their own," Cuncha said. "And they don't know how to behave."

"They certainly don't," said my mother.

"They don't understand anything," I said. "They must feel so alone. Each of them." I felt sorry for them, even if they were stingy.

43

"I'd like to be alone with all that rice and sugar and everything else they have," Cuncha said with a laugh. "But they have to stop being so stingy. I hope Nonti told them that."

"If he told them, the giant one wrote it down in that stupid orange notebook," my mother said.

"Those old ladies have three entire cracker tins full of crackers," Chawa announced to my mother.

"Hanso! You lie! Cracker tins full of crackers? Liar."

"Come see. They are arranging their things. Come see. You won't believe what they have."

We all have cracker tins to store our things in—our spun cotton, our unspun cotton, our beads, our thread, our needles. We buy them from the traders. And now here were these women with *new* cracker tins— complete with fresh crackers.

A few women had already gathered at Chawa's. We all stood around, watching them sort out more wealth than any of us had ever dreamed of. Teolinda, my mother's brother's wife, turned to me and said, "Give me that little nawa runt. I'll feed her. Mine is asleep." She took her baby out of her sling and laid her down on a mat next to her. I handed her my baby. She looked so beautiful. Her forehead was beginning to be flattened,

44

and Nachi was right. Her eyebrows were lovely. My beautiful daughter.

"Her name is Cami," I said.

"Hmm, hmm," said Teolinda. "Whatever it would be."

The old ladies just kept working at packing and unpacking, not paying us any attention.

"Look at all that stuff," said Elena. "I have never seen so much stuff, even in the store I went into in Pucallpa."

"Maybe they are going to set up a store here," said Teolinda. "And maybe their prices will be better than those thieving regatónes who come up our river."

"Maybe they'll sell beer—maybe cold beer. And candy and cloth to make blouses and beautiful colored thread to weave and maybe ice cream!"

We laughed at Shonta. She was Chawa's oldest daughter, younger than me, and she had the best imagination.

"And how will they make beer cold, you silly goose?" asked her mother. "There is no such thing as cold beer. And there is no ice cream. Ice cream is a made-up thing. It is all nawa talk, nawa talk to make you think there is something better out there. Lies, it is all lies." Chawa didn't believe anything she hadn't seen with her own eyes or touched with her own fingers. She certainly didn't believe in cold. I had been to Pucallpa and I knew about cold beer and ice cream. Many of us knew. But Chawa didn't believe anyone. She thought that nawa cast spells on people when they were out of their own villages and could make them believe anything.

"Look at how much sugar they have!" my mother said. "Sacks of sugar. And just as much rice. Maybe they are planning a dinner for the whole village."

"I doubt it," said Chawa. "They only hoard things. They haven't given me anything since they got here. I made a big deer stew for them for dinner and they didn't even give me any rice to add to it. They give me a cup of coffee after dinner each evening, and one for breakfast. But that's it."

"Chawa, you liar, they gave you beads," my mother said. "Look at those new beads she is wearing. They are so red. Hoshin shama. Very red. Take off your beads and let us see if you strung them well."

Chawa took off her big necklace and laid it out on the floor.

"What kind of beads are these? They look like candy," she said, shrugging.

In the midst of the rest of Chawa's beads, they looked

beautiful, like newly ripened berries on an old, drab bush.

"So they gave me beads. Strange beads," she went on. "But I am going to be feeding them for a long time. Look at their house. Only the postholes are dug. And there is no flooring. It will take a long time before that house is finished. And I will have no bananas to feed my family because these old ladies will eat up everything."

"Do they have more beads?" my mother asked.

"Tins full of them," said Chawa. "Tins and tins, *full* of beads. They brought them from their country to trade for our things. Some are really beautiful."

"I'm going to get some old bowls I made. Maybe they'll trade with me," my mother announced. She stood up and marched back toward our house.

I had nothing to trade. I had never fired any of the bowls I had shaped, and the only skirt I had made myself was the one I was wearing.

"Here's your little nawa. She has a good appetite," said Teolinda as she handed her back to me. "I have an old pisha that is almost finished. Maybe they'll trade me." She stood up and walked toward her house.

"I am not leaving," said Leoncia, Teolinda's co-wife. "I want to see everything I can see. Maybe they do have

47

some ice cream that they are hiding. That's what I want. Ice cream."

"Ice cream and turtles that fly. You'll wait a long time then," Chawa laughed.

"Look. Those are rifle cartridges. Boxes and boxes of them. We will all get fat now," said Leoncia. "Our husbands will bring in enough meat to feed us four meals a day. All meat. Sleep, little one," she whispered to her baby in her sling. "You will grow up nice and beautiful and fat, thanks to these two old ladies. And then you will marry a handsome hunter who will be bewitched by your fat beauty and bring you much meat, forever."

Maybe these old ladies would not be stingy with me. Maybe these old ladies would help me feed my Cami. Maybe they would help me save her. Cami wriggled in my sling. I patted her shoulder, and she cooed. She was looking so much better than when I first took her. No one but Nachi and I seemed to notice how beautiful she was.

My mother and Teolinda returned, my mother with a drinking bowl, Teolinda with a man's bag with no papiti, no strap. Teolinda thrust the bag under Margarita's nose.

"Oinhue. Nato pisha hacon shama," Teolinda said.

Margarita looked at the pisha. "Hacon shama icha," she said, smiling at Teolinda. All the women laughed. Margarita had said, "Very nice muchly." But Margarita liked the pisha. She took it in her hand and traced the design Teolinda had painted.

"Hahueti copi?" Margarita asked correctly. How much is it?

"Hahueti raibirai," Teolinda answered. However much it would be.

Margarita called Joanna to come and look at the pisha. "Icha hacon shama," said Joanna. Muchly very nice.

They talked to each other a little bit and finally Margarita said, "Teoti raveu." Two necklaces!

Teolinda nodded and nodded. She was very happy. Two necklaces!

"Get them to show you the necklaces," my mother said to her. "Don't let go of that pisha until you see the necklaces."

Margarita was digging around in one of the tins and came up with two little bags full of shiny beads. She handed the bags to Teolinda.

"She meant beads, not necklaces," my mother said. "The beads are very nice. Take them."

Teolinda took the beads and said to my mother, "They didn't even care that there is no papiti."

49

"Maybe they are not so stingy," Elena said.

"Maybe and maybe not," my mother said. "They are nawa. We will wait and see."

My mother showed her drinking bowl to Margarita. "Hacon. Hacon shama," my mother said.

"Hacon," said Margarita. "Hacon."

My mother looked at me and giggled. "It's one of my worst. I was going to throw this one away. Look how ugly the design is. I was trying something new and it didn't work." To Margarita she said, "Ravue. Ravue teoti. Teolinda quesca." And to me, "Do you think they will really give me two bags of beads for this ugly old bowl?"

Margarita dug into her tin again and gave my mother two bags of beads. By this time, every woman in the village was going home to see what old things they had around to trade for two bags of beads. Women came with old bowls, bowls that hadn't been glazed, half-started skirts, cushmas, pishas, necklaces, and bracelets. Anything they could think of.

I wished I did not let my mother do everything for me; I wished I had made some skirts or bowls or bags to trade with the old ladies. I wanted some of those beads.

Margarita bought a few more things, and Joanna

bought a bowl, but by now their house was overflowing with women. And some of the women started opening up the cracker tins and looking through all the old ladies' things. At first, the old ladies laughed and moved the tins farther away. But the women were everywhere, and they were going through everything. Margarita began yelling at us to stop, to go away. Joanna said nothing, but her mouth was pinched and she twirled her fish ring.

"Elena, you thought they would not be stingy," my mother said. "You were wrong. They are worse than any nawa I ever met. They have so much, and they give nothing."

She was right. They had so many beads and they didn't even wear them. What was wrong with them?

A few of the women had managed to take some bags of beads, hide them in their shawls, and pass more bags of beads to their kinswomen. We all took beads. I got a bag full of tiny little white ones. They were very odd. They looked like babies' teeth.

For a few days after the day of the beads, every person in the village stopped by the old ladies' house to get some beads. Men asked for beads for their wives, women asked for themselves, children asked for their mothers.

"There are no more beads," the old ladies would say. "They are all gone. You have taken them all."

"Where are *my* beads? Why should everyone else have new beads but me?" No woman would admit that she had taken any beads, or that anyone had given her any. But the truth was, there were no beads left. And the old ladies were really mad about that.

"What did they think?" my mother said. "Did they think they could live here and keep tins and tins full of beads that all of us wanted just sitting there in front of us? They brought more beads than anyone could ever use. And they don't even wear them! Why are they so mad? They brought the beads for us. And now we have them."

CHAPTER SEVEN Soon after the day of the beads, the old ladies began to do two things. First, they told everyone to come and ask for medicines. They had eye-drops for infected eyes, aspirina for pain, paregorico for diarrhea, a white cream and some blood-red liquid that burned for sores, and antibióticos for very bad sores. They would wait in Chawa's house each morning, and people could come and get medicine. That was good. The second thing they began to do was not so good. They started to walk through the village every evening to visit every house. They visited all eighteen houses. They didn't seem to notice that no one else ever did that. No one visits everybody. You visit someone. You don't stroll through the whole village. These women knew nothing about manners. They just burst into someone's house, no matter if it was mealtime. For normal people, if you happened to arrive at someone's house when they were starting to eat, they invited you to join the meal. But if that happened, or if you were really hungry and you arrived at mealtime on purpose, you knew you had to pay them back. You expected to see these people who had fed you arrive at your house for a meal. That is the way things are done. But these women! They wandered through the village at a time when everyone was eating, and they said, "No, thank you. We're not hungry." Then why were they walking around when people are eating?

Juanita and her sister decided to teach them a lesson. They found out that Margarita had traded some bullets to Nimeran so when he went hunting the next time he would bring the old ladies a piece of whatever he got. And Nimeran had just returned with a nice big deer. The old ladies got a leg. Chawa cooked it for them, and when they were shooing the chickens out of their kitchen so they could sit down and eat, Juanita and her sister arrived to "visit." Chawa, of course, knew what was going on. She also knew that Margarita and Joanna were starving. They hadn't eaten meat for at least a week. I watched from my house, swinging my little Cami in her hammock. My mother watched too. Cami was watching her fingers, as she always did just before she fell asleep. She held her little hands up right in front of her eyes, as if she were a little old half-blind lady, and stared at her fingers wiggling. She would do that until her falling eyelids fluttered and stayed closed.

"Hohue," Joanna said to Juanita and Paulita. At least she had learned the appropriate greeting.

"Hoho," they both responded, leaning up against the kitchen posts, looking down at the bowls full of wonderful-smelling deer stew.

"I don't know if they'll invite you to eat or not," said Chawa. "When they're hungry, they are animals. Joanna practically grabbed the last piece of turtle meat from my little one the other day. They have no manners and very little sense. And they give me and my children nothing."

"Well, we'll just see what happens," said Paulita. And they both continued to lean up against the kitchen poles. Joanna started to look uncomfortable and said something to Margarita, who seemed to be thinking it over, whatever it was. Then they both came to some understanding, and Margarita said to Juanita and Paulita, "Sit, eat. Pihue!"

"Maybe they are beginning to learn something," Chawa said to Juanita, as Juanita dipped her fingers into the big stew bowl. Joanna got two more spoons from the kitchen shelf and handed one to each of the visitors. The old ladies never ate with their fingers and seemed not to understand why we did. Some of us had a few spoons, but we hardly ever used them. Fingers are so much easier, and none of us mind the heat of the stew.

"I guess they're not always as stingy as they are most of the time," my mother said.

"At least they're interesting. And they are fun to watch," said Chawa.

And the whole village seemed to agree. They were fun to watch.

The next morning the old ladies brought oatmeal to the men working on their house. In the afternoon they put on smiles and walked toward my house.

"Hohue," my mother said. "Alicia, tell them to sit down and let you pick their heads. Then tell them to give you some sugar for your skinny nawa."

Maybe they would stop being so stingy if I helped them. I knew they were suffering from the lice.

"Sit down and I'll pick the lice from your head," I said.

Joanna was happy. "Icha ia," she said. "I have lots of lice."

She certainly did. "Look," I said to my mother, as I parted Joanna's long hair. "Have you ever seen so many?"

There were lice crawling up and down every strand of her hair. No matter where you looked on Joanna's head, something moved.

"The one thing she is not stingy about," said my mother.

I lit my pipe and blew smoke all over her head. "It helps kill the lice," I explained. And then I proceeded to go through her hair, section by section, pulling out more lice than I had ever seen on one head. Joanna sat very still. Her hair was very soft. My mother started to work on Margarita's head. It was almost as bad as Joanna's.

Cami was lying on the mat next to me. She was lying on her back, kicking her arms and legs, wriggling to get her arms up so that her fingers would be right in front of her face.

"How old is your baby?" Joanna asked.

"I don't know. I took her while you were gone."

"Took her?"

"Yes. I took her, you know, adopted her. She is a nawa," I said, and told them the story of how I adopted my little Cami.

Joanna's eyes got big. "But how do you feed her? How do you keep her alive?" she asked.

"I pass her around to my kinswomen who have milk. Sometimes my mother nurses her, sometimes I give her chapo. I drip it into her little mouth. But she is always hungry."

"She is so beautiful," Joanna said. "And you have flattened her forehead. She looks like an Isabo. A beautiful Isabo baby."

Only Nachi had said how beautiful she was. And now Joanna.

"She is very beautiful," Margarita agreed. "Look at those wonderful eyelashes. They are so long."

"Ask for some of their food," my mother said to me. "Ask them now."

This was hard. *They* should have thought to offer me food for the baby. I shouldn't have to ask. But they didn't know how to behave. So I was forced to ask. That was bad enough. But I was sure they would say no, like they always did. To ask and be told no is the worst insult.

"Mama, they will say no. I don't want to ask," I said quickly to my mother.

"They are nawa," my mother growled. "Do not think of them as people. It doesn't matter if they say no. It

58

means nothing. Only that they are stingy. Ask. They will never give on their own."

"Give me some of your sugar to feed her," I said to Joanna. "She is very hungry." I thought Joanna might not be as stingy as Margarita. I hoped.

Joanna looked at Margarita. Margarita got that look on her face, the look she always got when she was about to say no. But then Joanna started talking fast, turning her silver fish ring, and Margarita's face softened.

"I'll give you some later," said Joanna. "Come to our house in the evening."

"Stingy old ladies," my mother muttered. "They will give you nothing."

That evening while they sat outside their kitchen, enjoying the sunset, I went to their house, carrying my Cami in my sling. Joanna put her arms out.

"Can I hold her?" she asked me.

"Yes," I said. I handed Cami to her.

"She's so light," said Joanna. "Like a feather." Joanna held her cradled in both arms. She looked down at Cami and smiled.

"Alicia," she said. "She is so sweet. Look, she is smiling at me."

Cami stuck her tongue out. Joanna stuck her tongue out. Cami smiled.

"She is so sweet, so sweet. Like sugar," said Joanna. And then she sang to Cami. She sang softly, in her own language. "It's a song about being as sweet as sugar," she said when she finished. "My mother used to sing it to me."

Margarita reached for the baby. Joanna took a big plastic bag filled with sugar from inside one of their cooking pots. She tucked it into my sling quickly and looked around to see if anyone had seen her do it. At last she was not being stingy and she wanted to keep it a secret!

"Whenever you need sugar for Cami, just ask me," she whispered. "I will always save some for her."

"I will," I said. Maybe someday she would learn to just give it to me, without my having to ask.

I took Cami back and sat down. I felt the bag of sugar in my sling. It was a big bag. It would be enough sugar for Cami for days and days. Cami was making her new gurgly sounds, moving her tongue in and out and around her mouth.

"Tell us about your caibo," Joanna said. "Tell us what you call your relatives. What you call your sister."

"My sister is my sister," I said. My huetsa.

"But you also call Wishtin your sister, right?" Margarita had her orange notebook and her pen ready.

"Yes. [Wishtin is my mother's mother's sister's daughter's daughter's daughter.] But since my father had sex with her mother just before Wishtin was born, we could call each other sister. Not, of course, if Wishtin's father was around to hear that."

"Why not?" Margarita asked.

"Why not?" Didn't they know? I tried talking very slowly to them. "Men like to think they are the only fathers of their children. They don't like to think that some other man or some other men helped to create their children." But of course that is what happens. Which is good, since everyone knows it takes a lot of sex to make a baby.

"What do you mean?" Joanna asked.

No wonder they had no children! "Every time a man has sex with a woman, this stuff comes out of his penis and goes into her vagina," I explained.

"Yes," Joanna said. "We know that."

"Well, that's the stuff that makes babies. You need a lot of that stuff to make a baby and to keep it growing so it will be born healthy."

"I see. So it's good to have a lot of sex, it makes healthier babies?"

61

"Of course. And it's good to have sex with a few men—not too many—because the stuff from a few different men all goes to create a nice big baby."

They were astounded. "You mean that many different men can be father to one child?"

"Of course," I said. I felt like I was talking to two infants. "Didn't you know that?"

"But why do you say not to have sex with too many men? What is too many? Why is that bad?"

"Too many is more than three or four. Each father must obey the taboos, or his baby will be harmed."

"What taboos?"

They did not know anything. "Men must not do hard work when their babies are still young. And they must not eat white monkey, or tapir," I said. "If they do, the baby will die. Too many fathers, one is sure to make a mistake. One is sure to do something to harm his child."

Cami started to cry.

"She's hungry. I'll take her to my mother to feed her," I said, and went home. I was tired of their questions. They knew so little and they asked so much.

CHAPTER EIGHT These women were going to study babies! They didn't even understand how to make one. Unbelievable. And they didn't know the first thing about cleanliness. When they first arrived, they did not bathe at all—for at least two days, maybe more. I couldn't believe it. None of us could believe it. They didn't bathe in the morning and they didn't bathe in the evening. And they went behind the houses into the jungle to do their business. We were horrified at that. It was bad enough that they were dirty themselves. But they were making our jungle dirty too. Someone must have told them, for soon they were going to the river, just like us, to do their business. But no one had told them to face upstream. They learned that the hard way one morning, when grandmother Yoshran had bad diarrhea. From then on, they always faced upstream.

They did learn to go down to the river in the morning to bathe, just like everyone else, using just the section of river right in front of their kitchen. But they didn't bathe like everyone else. They would finish and come up the bank, proud as young hunters returning with their first big game, acting as if they were clean—and they hadn't gotten a single hair on their heads wet! Not a drop. In fact, they tied their hair up on top of their heads to *keep it* from getting wet. They just got their bodies wet.

"They are filthy, like all nawa," my mother said.

I didn't know how to tell them, but I felt I had to. They were trying to do things right. Someone had to tell them what was wrong. I tried to get Elena to do it, but she liked watching their strange ways. She didn't want them to change.

Joanna was in their house. I walked over and sat down, Cami asleep in my sling.

"Is cleanliness important where you come from?" I decided to begin gradually. It was still morning, but it was after the sun had been up long enough to chase away the mosquitoes. Now the gnats were plentiful.

"Oh, yes. Very important," Joanna told me, swatting at the pesky little gnats. "Every morning I take a shower before I get dressed. Every morning. And most of my countrymen do the same."

"What's a shower?" I asked her.

"We have a room in our houses called bathrooms," she continued. "In the bathroom is a toilet, a sink, and a bathtub and shower. The toilet is a thing you sit on to do your daily business—both kinds—and the sink has a spout where water comes out so you can wash your hands, and the tub or shower is a bigger sink where a lot of water can come out of a bigger, taller spout so you can wash yourself." She pantomimed water coming from high over her head, and swatted a few gnats as she pretended that water was trickling down.

"How does the water get *into* your house?" I asked. They had shown me pictures of their houses, their apartments, all piled on top of one another somehow.

Joanna looked puzzled. "I don't know," she said. "I can't explain it. There's a lot about the way we live that I can't explain. But it's true anyway." She looked uncomfortable. I didn't think she was lying. Why should she? But I didn't understand. How could she not understand how water came into her own house?

"How far away from the river do you live?" I asked.

"Oh, not far." Joanna started to answer me and then stopped. She waved her hand in front of her face to make the gnats go away. They didn't. "But the water that comes into our houses doesn't come from the river."

Now she had to be lying. "Where does it come from?" I asked. I was waiting for a really incredible story.

"Well, it comes from a big lake that is called a reservoir. The reservoir for our house is far, far away."

"How many days by canoe?" I asked.

"Oh, maybe two days by canoe. But no one has a canoe. The water in the reservoir is sent through great big pipes under the ground and then smaller pipes take that water from those bigger pipes and send it to everyone's house."

I didn't know what she meant about water being "sent." Who sent it? Pipes can't just push water around. But there was another part of this that made even less sense.

"But how does it get *up* into your house, way up there in the air?"

"I don't know," said Joanna. "I really don't know. It doesn't make any sense to me either, but it happens. That's the way we do things there. It's our custom."

"Oh," I said. I had almost forgotten why I had started this conversation.

"Cleanliness is important to us too," I began. "And we have noticed that you go down to the river to bathe every morning, just like we do, and that is good, but there is one thing that people have begun to worry about." I was talking fast because I didn't want to be interrupted by Joanna's questions. "So while it is good that you have begun to do as we do, there is one part of the bathing that you don't seem to understand."

"What could that be?" asked Joanna, turning her fish ring.

"You never get your hair wet. You go down to the river and dunk yourselves in and you even take soap with you, but when you come back up your hair is always dry. You never get your hair wet."

"But I wash my hair in the afternoon, in the afternoon when we go to bathe," said Joanna.

"But you are dirty in the morning. Dirty at the most important bath time. Dirty to begin the day. That is why people have been laughing at you in the morning."

"I wondered why that was," Joanna said. "I thought they were just happy that we had finally started bathing twice a day, like you all do." She looked sad. I had never seen her look sad before.

"I'm sorry, I just wanted you to know."

"It's okay." She smiled. "Live and learn. There is so much we don't know."

She was right about that. At least she was learning something. I smiled back, and waved my shawl around her head to chase away the gnats.

I know she explained this to Margarita later, after Margarita returned from measuring gardens or whatever she had been doing that morning. The next morning they both came up from the river with their hair very wet.

"Look, they have decided to act like real people," my mother said. "They must want something from us."

The old ladies were so happy when everyone smiled at them. They seemed pleased to have done the right thing. They want to be liked, it is important to them that we like them, I thought. I had never thought that it mattered to them. But they were so happy to have learned how to behave properly. They paraded up the riverbank, shaking their long wet hair so that no one could miss how wet it was. And it made me feel good that they cared, that it mattered to them what we thought.

CHAPTER NINE That night, long after everyone was asleep, I heard voices from the old ladies' house. I sat up and could see them through their mosquito net. They had one of their candles lit, and their voices were louder than usual. And they sounded different—not like their usual conversations. Chawa had taken her children to Weesoshando to visit her sister. The old ladies were alone, and something was wrong.

I picked up my little Cami, wrapped my shawl around my shoulders, and tiptoed over to their house, swatting the mosquitoes away from my sleeping baby's head. Margarita seemed to be rolling all over the floor, while Joanna kept looking through a book and reading aloud from it. Then she dropped the book, moved over, and hugged Margarita tightly. Margarita was moaning and crying. I walked in. Joanna was pale, and her eyes were big as a wild peccary's.

"What do you want?" Joanna snapped. "I have nothing to give you."

Joanna had never spoken like this, so angry, so cruel.

"What's the matter?" I asked. "What's the matter with you?"

"It's Margarita," she said. "I'm sorry. She is sick. She has a very bad stomachache," she said. "I'm trying to figure out what is wrong with her. This is a book about medicine from my country. It will tell me what to do. She has already thrown up every pill we have." Joanna was speaking very fast, as if she was in a rush to go someplace else and had to finish talking first. There was a big cooking pot next to Margarita that, I knew from the smell, held everything Margarita had thrown up.

Margarita looked really sick. I had never seen a sick white person, but I had seen a lot of sick kinsmen, and Margarita was sick. She was only throwing up now, but it could be just the beginning. She could have the throwing up and diarrhea sickness, and die very quickly. I hugged my nawa closer. I was furious at Joanna. Why hadn't she asked for help?

"How could you sit here and read to her? She needs

70

to be cured. So she isn't your kinswoman, so what? She needs you to help her, she needs to be cured."

Joanna stared at me.

"What's the matter with you?" I asked her. "Why didn't you call Papaisi? He can cure her in a minute." Cami started to cry. I put my finger in her mouth, and she gnawed at it. Joanna stared at me. Now her eyes were like a dead peccary's.

"I will get Papaisi." I left the old ladies and went to Papaisi's house. I woke him up and told him that those two old ladies were trying to cure Margarita out of a book! He was astounded—and insulted. He grabbed his pipe and came with me. As he stepped into their house, he took charge.

"Don't worry," he said to Joanna. "I will cure her."

What was the matter with Joanna? She had just sat there for I don't know how long, while Margarita moaned and writhed in pain, and had just read her book.

Papaisi led Margarita out on the porch and told her to lie on her back. I brought the candle from inside their mosquito net out to the porch so he could see what he was doing. He stroked her stomach until he felt where the spirit had lodged. "Aha, here it is," he said. By now, the whole village had gathered on the porch to watch. Papaisi started smoking his pipe, inhaling and swallowing the smoke, holding some in his mouth. When he had enough, he placed his mouth on the place where the spirit was in Margarita's belly, and he coaxed it out. He swirled the smoke all around the area, and when the spirit came out and entered his mouth, he bit Margarita's stomach to seal off the hole it had come from, so that the spirit couldn't enter Margarita again. Then he leaned over the side of the porch and vomited the spirit out. Cami stopped chewing on my finger and slept.

"Ah," we all sighed in relief. "Rambi yoshin. Cahue, yoshin." It was done. It was over. The spirit was gone, and Margarita was cured. We all knew that, but Joanna still looked worried. Then Margarita sat up, looked around at us all, looked at Joanna, and told her, "It's gone. It's all gone. What happened?" And then she smiled. And Joanna burst into tears.

"You should have called him earlier, you bad old woman," I told her.

"Next time I will, I promise," she said, and hugged me and patted Cami's little head. "I'm sorry. You are right. I'm sorry I yelled at you. You were being kind. I was so scared. Next time I will call you." She kept hugging me and crying.

"Give Papaisi some cigarettes," I whispered to her. "Now is not the time to be stingy." The old man was waiting around, and I knew he was tired and wanted to go back to bed.

"Just cigarettes? Is that enough?" Joanna asked.

"Yes, that's fine," I said.

Joanna got a whole pack of cigarettes and gave them to Papaisi. Good for her. While she was hugging him and thanking him he said, "Do you think you could give me about four of those white pills of yours, the ones for pain? My stomach is hurting me very much tonight."

Joanna laughed and got four white pills from their big medicine box. "Aspirina," she said.

I was glad Papaisi cured Margarita. I was glad that it was Papaisi, not Joanna with her book. It gave both the old ladies a respect for us that they had not had before. I think it affected Joanna even more than Margarita. She had been the more worried one, and she had been the one to do nothing, to not ask for the help she needed. Margarita had been so sick that she wasn't thinking much about anything. But Joanna, I knew, had been thinking about death. And Papaisi had saved her friend from death, from death far away from home, among people who didn't know her or love her. At least Margarita would have been dead—Joanna would have had to face life even more alone than she had been. And I knew that she would have thought it was her fault that her friend died. I knew that. I can't explain how I knew it, but I knew it. She was wrong, of course. It was the spirit Margarita had encountered up the creek when she had gone poison fishing. Papaisi said so. It was a tree spirit that had made her sick. But I knew Joanna didn't believe that.

"Why do you think Margarita got sick?" I asked Joanna when she came to my house to watch me make pots. I had just fed Cami a big meal of chapo with some of the old ladies' sugar, and she was sound asleep in her hammock.

"Why? I don't know. I know Papaisi thinks it was a tree spirit. But why would a tree spirit want to harm Margarita? It doesn't make sense to me."

"Do you think it is your fault?" I loved pretending I was Joanna—asking her as many questions as she asked.

She looked surprised. "Well, I guess I do. I guess I do. I certainly would have blamed myself if she had died."

I nodded. These women blamed everything bad that happened on themselves, or sometimes on each other. They never talked about gods or spirits. How could it

74

be a person's fault that another person died? I mean, just an everyday, normal person, not a witch. Joanna had not cast a spell on Margarita, or gone to Shori to cast the spell. So how could it be her fault?

"You don't think that way, do you?" she asked me.

"No. It really was a tree spirit. How can you think you have such power, to be able to harm people? No, it can't be. Only if you ate a tabooed food, or asked a witch to cast a spell. People don't have that kind of power over each other by accident, by chance, for no reason, without spending much time learning to be a witch. No. You can only harm other people if you mean to."

Joanna took a piece of clay and tried to roll a coil, as I was doing. She wasn't very good. She kept stopping and looking out at the river. She was thinking about something.

"You know," she said, "when my mother died, I used to have horrible dreams that I had killed her. I would dream I had a gun and I shot her, just like that, for no reason."

We all knew that Joanna's mother had died when she was little. Joanna had told us.

"But you didn't kill her," I said. "You didn't even make her sick. You couldn't. You were a child."

"I knew that. I knew in my mind that I hadn't killed her, but in my heart, way inside, I believed. I believed it was my fault she died." Joanna stared at the river, at the forest on the other side.

We sat silently.

"I guess it's time I believed what my mind knows," she said. "But it's hard. It's hard to change your heart." She looked at me. "Learning from you, learning what you know, helps."

"Good," I said. I wished she would learn so easily when it came to stinginess.

Only a few men were working on the old ladies' house the next morning. Most were out hunting. Elena came by later in the day and sat with me. "I have a great story to tell you about my students, the old ladies," she said with a laugh.

"Good," I said. "A laugh would feel good in my empty belly." There had been no meat in the village for a few days.

"Listen to this. I thought they were learning our language really well, but then this morning lots of children came over to look at all the pictures they have, and Margarita wanted them to leave. I had taught them to say, 'Catanhue baquebo. Matonra ea hatsain.' Margarita said that. She said it correctly, 'Go away, children. You are bothering me.' And of course the children stayed there and told her how well she was learning to speak Isabo. So finally Joanna stood up, picked up her machete, and announced in a big voice, 'Era shevi acai!'" Elena and I laughed and laughed. Joanna had been trying to say, "I am going out to make grass"—to clear out the grass around her house—but the word for grass is shovi, not shevi. Shevi means vagina.

"So now all the children tease Joanna unmercifully, 'Shevi shovi shevi shovi. Which is which, Joanna?'" Elena said. This story would be told all through the village by evening. Elena stopped speaking and looked away.

"Is something wrong?" I asked her.

"I don't know. Maybe I'm just hungry. The old ladies still have rice left, and they don't offer us any. And we haven't had any meat for days. Maybe that's all. It makes me mad to see them eating whatever they want while we are hungry."

"I know," I said. "Do you think they would let their own families go hungry? Maybe they were chased out of their own country for being stingy and that is why they have come here." I said nothing to Elena about the old ladies giving food to Cami. That was a secret. I had never had a secret from Elena before.

We sat there awhile, playing with Cami. When Cami cried, Elena picked her up and rocked her.

"She is growing bigger and bigger, although she is still a skinny thing," Elena said. Elena put her down in her hammock, and we drew designs in the dirt as we talked and pulled the hammock string.

"That's a nice one," Elena said about one I had just drawn.

"I'm thinking about making some painted skirts. I have been thinking about a nice big pattern to paint on them," I said.

Elena dusted away her design and started on another. "My brother goes out to the gardens every day with Margarita. She takes a big metal roll and has him measure the gardens with her. Who cares how big the garden is as long as it still yields bananas?" Elena rubbed out her design and then relaxed a bit. "I should stop complaining. After all, they are paying me to teach them Isabo, and they are paying my brother to measure. But their money doesn't buy us meat."

CHAPTER TEN   That afternoon Nimeran came back with a big deer. We were so happy. My mother and I ran to his house to receive the intestines to make stew. But everyone was waiting for the deer to be weighed on the scale Margarita had given each hunter. Margarita wanted every piece of food that came into the village weighed! Each hunter had his own notebook to write down what kind of animal it was and how much it weighed. And Nimeran was doing that before he gave the deer to his wife to butcher.

"We are all hungry," said Micasio, Nimeran's wife. "At least let me start to butcher it. Let me give the intestines away so that a stew can start to cook. Who cares how much the intestines weigh?"

Nimeran was as hungry as the rest of us, so he let

Micasio butcher the deer first. My mother took the intestines home. Then Nimeran weighed all the rest of the deer before Micasio could give the pieces to her kinswomen, who were all standing around waiting for their share.

Nimeran took one leg and brought it to Margarita. She had given him cartridges to take on his hunting trip and so he owed her a piece. Micasio complained to all the women waiting for their share, "Why does he always give those old ones the biggest piece? There are only two of them and we are hungrier. Let them live on those fish they get in cans. Let them eat their crackers. They should not be taking the food out of my children's mouths."

Her children's mouths would have been empty without the cartridges Margarita gave Nimeran in the first place. And one leg was a fair exchange. But no one said that.

My mother's intestine stew was finished first. My brother, Marco, stood in the middle of the road between our kitchen and our house and shouted, "Pihue! Food is ready. Come and eat." All of my mother's caibo who lived in our neighborhood came right away, bringing their own plates. All the men and boys sat down on their haunches together just outside the kitchen. The women, girls, and small children all sat together inside the kitchen, right next to the fire. My mother's stew was delicious. She put big chunks of yuca in it, and a special spice that she uses. Everyone ate and ate. When we were almost finished, Nimeran stood in the road and told everyone that Micasio's stew was now ready. We all took our plates and went to Micasio's. It is so wonderful when a hunter brings in a deer. Deer are big and there is lots of food. Nimeran even took a big bowl of stew over to the old ladies, who were watching everything from their house, watching and writing in their notebooks. Micasio grumbled about wasting more food on them, but Nimeran ignored her and sat down to eat with the men.

Even when we have no meat, we do not starve. We always have our gardens, we always have whatever fruit and nuts are in season. But when a hunter comes home with meat, everyone feels full and happy, and it lasts for a few days, depending on how big the animal is. Meat hunger can only be satisfied by meat. No matter how many bananas or how much yuca you eat, you can still be hungry for meat. And when people are hungry for meat, they are not happy. When people have enough meat, everything else seems much better—your husband looks younger, almost handsome, your children smile

81

and look fat, your mother's requests don't seem so difficult to accomplish, your kinsmen seem generous, your brothers and sisters never act lazy, and the old people don't seem so close to death.

Even the old ladies seemed different—softer, happier, sillier. They were eating the stew Chawa had made from the deer leg Nimeran had brought them. And they were laughing as they ate, not asking questions and writing the answers down. They were just eating, like the rest of us. When they had finished, they came to Micasio's kitchen, where we were all finishing eating Micasio's stew. Margarita brought Nimeran a big cup of coffee with lots of sugar. Nimeran smiled up at Margarita as she handed him the coffee.

"Hainqui mia itai?" Are you here? Our standard greeting.

"Hain ea itai," Margarita answered correctly. I am here.

"Elena is doing a good job," said Nimeran. "Except for the grass/vagina day." He spoke too fast for Margarita to understand, but she smiled back at him anyway. I think she understood that everyone loved to talk about that Joanna story.

"Chasho hacon shama," said Margarita. The deer was very good. "Hacon biris." Very, very good.

"Chasho hacon." Nimeran agreed.

I expected her to start asking questions—how far did you have to go to find the deer, how many cartridges did you have to shoot, what other animals did you see on the trail, do you have to go farther from the village now than when you were young? But she didn't ask a thing. She offered Nimeran a cigarette, lit her own and then his, and just sat down and relaxed. She was human after all. She was usually so tense, so determined to write everything down, so tight in the lip, so serious.

"Meat is good," she said. "Meat makes people happy."

"Yes," said Nimeran. "Meat is very, very good. Without meat, a man is worthless. Without meat, he can have sex no more than once, maybe twice, a day. And he will probably pass out. But a well-fed man, a man who has eaten enough meat, he is good three, four, even five times a day."

"Yes," said Papaisi. "He does not lie. Meat is important."

That night, Joanna and Margarita played some of their own music on their tape recorder. They hardly ever did that. They were always saving their batteries. But that night they sang along with the tape recorder. The music was funny. It didn't sound like the music the missionaries played, and it didn't sound like Peruvian music either. It sounded strange to me, but they seemed to love it. My brother and I were sitting in their house when they turned on the tape recorder. My mother was taking care of Cami.

"What does it say?" I asked.

"It says, 'The first days are the hardest days, don't you worry. Because when life looks easy, there is danger coming,'" said Joanna, and she smiled even though a tear came down.

That was a funny thing to sing about, I thought. First they sing a song about bananas that they say is not even a word in their language, and now this. We sing about being careful not to offend the spirits, making sure to be generous to your caibo, never to be lazy, what it was like in the very olden days, even before our grandparents lived, about the rivers, the big ones and the little ones.

Joanna dug around inside one of the many boxes they kept and took out a little box. She opened the little box and began pulling out a long piece of white string.

"What do you think she is doing with fish line now?" Marco asked me.

"We are all so full of meat, how can she even think about going fishing?" I told him.

The string looked strong, very strong. It would be

good to use to make bracelets—they would never fall apart. Joanna twirled the string around her fingers and began sticking it in between her teeth! Margarita took some and did the same. They each pulled out tiny pieces of food that stuck to the string.

"What are you doing?" I couldn't believe they were using such good, strong string to pull old pieces of food from their mouths.

"Cleaning our teeth. This is special string to clean in between the teeth. Here, try some," said Joanna as she handed me a long piece.

I pulled at it. It was really strong. Marco tried pulling at it too.

"Coshi. Coshi biris," I said. It's strong. I was right. It would be perfect for bracelets and necklaces. And Marco wanted some for fish line. It was stronger than any fish line he had ever had.

"Give us some, Joanna, for fish line," Marco pleaded.

"Give me some and I'll make bracelets for you that will never break," I said. "Your children will be able to wear such bracelets. Your grandchildren even." We were all trying to break the string and none of us could. This string, it was like no string I had ever seen. You couldn't break it.

"Here," said Joanna, and she handed us a whole little

box. "Just don't tell everyone. The whole village will be here asking us for dental floss."

In the morning, the whole village was asking them for the string—the floss, they called it. And this time they gave away a lot of it. But then they got mad when so many people kept coming to ask. I wondered what other treasures they had hidden in their boxes, treasures they did strange things with, treasures that we would put to good use.

CHAPTER ELEVEN Nonti was supposed to pick up the old ladies sometime soon and take them to Pucallpa for a time, a few weeks, they said. They had been with us since the beginning of the dry season. Now the rainy season was near. Their house was still not finished.

"Maybe they won't come back," my mother said. "How many more questions could they ask us? Let them go home to their own country and be stingy to their own caibo."

The old ladies were excited about leaving. They started packing up days before Nonti was due to arrive.

"What will you do in Pucallpa?" I asked Joanna.

"First, we will take showers," Joanna said. "Not hot showers, because they have no hot water at the hotel. But real showers. And then we will get dressed up and go out to dinner at a restaurant and order *cold* beer."

"Maybe a Scotch," Margarita chimed in, smiling and almost giggling. "A Scotch on the rocks," she added.

"That means a Scotch with ice," Joanna told me.

"Whatever ice is," I said. Joanna was not listening. She just went on.

"And then we will go out dancing and when we come home late at night, we can turn on the lights in our room and read or write or whatever. We will sleep in beds, with mattresses, and when we get up in the morning, we will take showers again. And go to a restaurant for breakfast. We will see all our friends in Pucallpa and pick up our mail from home and mail our letters to our friends and family in New York. And buy some newspapers and magazines and read about what has happened in the world while we have been here."

I had never seen her so excited. I didn't understand a lot of the things she told me, but she seemed so happy about them. I had been to Pucallpa three times, but I was an Isabo in Pucallpa. We stayed in our boat at the port. To be a gringo in Pucallpa would be something different. Maybe someday I would go with them on one of their visits, sleep on a bed, take a shower, drink cold beer, meet their friends, eat in a restaurant. It was hard to imagine these things. What would they be like then? Did they ask their own people as many questions as they asked us? Did they dance and laugh and not have their mouths so pinched?

"And then we will buy more supplies and come back here," Joanna was saying.

She and Margarita were getting ready to bathe. They took their soap and shampoo and started to go down to the river.

"Do you want to come with us and use our shampoo?" Joanna asked.

"Yes, I'll try it again," I said. I had tried it once, but I didn't like it very much. It smelled too sweet to me, and the gnats liked it too much.

"Here," Joanna whispered. She put a big plastic bag of sugar into my shawl. "For Cami," she told me. "Until we come back."

"Hacon," I said. Good. She had given without being asked!

We had fun washing one another's hair and backs. Some of the children came down too, and the old ladies gave shampoo to each child who asked. A bunch of white heads bobbing up and down in the muddy river.

"Rollin' on the river," sang Joanna. We all sang

with her, although we did not understand what we were singing. "Big wheel keep on turnin', Proud Mary keep on burnin'. . . ."

We all came up the riverbank, clean and singing. My mother was nursing my Cami while she stirred our fire. She looked at me as I came up.

"Nawa songs," I heard her mutter. "Listen to your mother, little one. She is learning nawa songs to sing to you. Nawa songs. Music with no meaning."

Chawa was starting to prepare dinner for the old ladies, and I stopped in the kitchen to talk with her.

"They are in such good moods," I said, looking at Chawa's house. The old ladies were still singing as they brushed their wet hair.

"I know," said Cuncha, who sat down with us. "They have been singing and packing and laughing and packing. I wonder if they are planning to come back at all."

"I think they are beginning to like it here," I said. Joanna had said so. She said she was learning so much.

"Maybe they have everything they need already," Chawa sighed. She wanted them to come back. She earned money being their cook. She also wanted their house to remain unfinished. Once it was built, it would be Cuncha who earned that money.

"Some people say they are too stingy with everything they have," Cuncha said, "that it is too hard on the village to have them here."

"They are stingy," said Chawa. "They live in my house and give me nothing. See how skinny my daughter is. And how fat that Joanna is. Now look at them. Now they are being crazy again."

I looked at the old ladies' section of Chawa's house. Margarita and Joanna were searching through everything, tearing up all their neat packages looking for something And they were not laughing.

"My watch is gone!" Margarita yelled to us.

Joanna patted her on the shoulder and talked loudly but calmly in their language. But Margarita was madder than I had ever seen her.

"Did someone steal it?" I asked Cuncha.

"Probably," Cuncha said. "Someone who doesn't want them to ever come back."

"Maybe Margarita just misplaced it."

"I don't think so," said Cuncha. "People are angry at them now that they are going and no one knows if they will return. They have promised to bring things back for some people and not others. They promised to bring Chawa a big cooking pot, but they promised nothing to Nachi. They promised cloth to Juanita and nothing to Paulita. I suppose stealing the watch is one way to make sure you get something from them."

Margarita was furious. She marched over to the teacher's house and told him that her watch had been stolen. Angel knew, of course. Everyone knew by now.

"It was Paviki, you know," Cuncha whispered to me. "Paviki, that little thief. He steals everything. He is a rat. He will grow up to be a big rat, just like his mother."

Paviki was Chawa's son and had been caught stealing pencils from all the other children at school.

"I am sure you have just misplaced it," said Angel. "I will help you look for it."

"I have not misplaced it," Margarita shouted. "Come and see. It is gone."

Angel came to see. "Where was the watch the last time you saw it?" he asked Margarita.

"Right here, on the floor. I always put it here when I go bathe. See? It is not here."

"And you took it off and put it right here?"

"Yes," said Margarita. She was still furious, but she was trying hard not to yell. "Right here where I always put it."

"And you went to bathe, you and Joanna?"

"Yes, Joanna and Alicia and many children. And we took soap and shampoo, but what difference does that make? The point is, my watch is gone. The point is, my watch has been stolen!"

"And when you came back up from bathing, did you come directly here or did you stop at someone else's house?"

"What difference does it make? I don't know, I think I just came home. AND THE WATCH WAS NOT HERE!"

Papaisi arrived just then. "Where was the watch the last time you saw it?" he asked Margarita.

Margarita stared at Papaisi, told him to ask Angel anything he wanted, and marched off into the jungle.

"She is upset," said Joanna, turning her fish ring.

At the river, a regatón arrived with a lot of liquor and not much else, but no one had any money. Only the old ladies.

"Go ask the old ladies for money," my mother yelled to Angel. "They are so giving. They still have that bottle left from their arrival party. They will give you that bottle and then I am sure they will give you money for more. They love to show how they are not stingy. Remember the day of the beads? And how generous they were with their string, their floss! Go, go ask them, unless you fear for your life!" My mother laughed and laughed.

That afternoon, Angel blew the horn and everyone started gathering in front of Chawa's house, on the old ladies' side.

Angel began the sesión by asking Margarita for the bill of sale for the watch. Angel had been to Pucallpa often and knew about buying things. Margarita didn't understand, and Angel had to repeat his question again and again. Finally she said, "I have no bill. I bought the watch years ago."

"If it is so old, why do you care about it?"

"Just go buy a new one."

"Someone from Weesoshando stole it. We do not do such things here."

"I did it. I stole the watch," Nimeran said. "Last night, when I sneaked in here to have sex with the two old ladies. Afterward I stole the watch." He could always make everyone laugh.

"The watch will reappear, we are sure of it," said Angel, and the meeting was over.

The watch did reappear that evening, in the exact spot it had disappeared from. Everyone came over to see.

"Now they should have a party," my mother said.

"Now that they have their precious watch back. Ask them, go ahead. They have their watch back and they will *still* be stingy. You'll see."

"Now is the time for a party. To celebrate the watch's return," Angel said to the old ladies. "Now that the village is happy again."

"A party?" Margarita was still angry. Even Joanna got angry about the idea of a party. They went into their mosquito net, opened their books, and wouldn't come out.

"You are right, old woman," Angel said to my mother. "The village found the watch and now these women won't even give a party to thank us. They grow meaner and meaner and stingier and stingier."

It was true. Even though we told them all the time, they just didn't know what was right. They were like babies who want everything for themselves and don't care about anyone else. They had different beliefs, and that made them act oddly. After all, Joanna believed she had killed her own mother!

That night, Angel blew the horn to announce another sesión. Everybody had begun grumbling about the old ladies. On my way, I yelled to them to come.

"We need to finish packing," Margarita called back.

95

"They are probably staying home to steal from us while we are all at the meeting," my mother said as she walked by their house, carrying my sleeping Cami.

So they weren't in front of Angel's house to hear all the complaints about them.

"Why do we want them here?" Angel asked. "What good do they do us? They are selfish and stingy. When we are hungry, they do not feed us, but they feed themselves. Let us tell them not to return."

"No. We told them when they first asked that they could live here," said Papaisi.

"We also told them that we would build them a house," said Nimeran. Everyone laughed.

"This is different," said Papaisi. "And we have been working on the house," he added. "Some of us."

"And some of us have been out hunting, trying to bring home meat for our families," said Eosario. "What do I care if those old ladies have a house? My wives and children need food, that is what I care about. Not whether some old white ladies get their watch back or have their own separate house."

A lot of people agreed with Eosario. There was no good reason to put up with these old ladies. They were not part of our lives, they were not our caibo. They were nothing to us. And besides, they were stingy.

They had brought many, many things with them and shared none. All this was true. The village had no good reason to keep them.

But I wanted them to stay. I didn't know why. Maybe I was just getting used to them—getting used to seeing them come up happy and wet from their baths in the morning, answering their questions, listening to their music, hearing about their country, sharing their shampoo in the afternoon, asking them questions. Yes. I was getting used to them, and I would miss them if they were not here. They were different now, different than the strangers they had been at first. Now they were real people, not caibo, but not nawa anymore. Like Cami. At first she was a nawa baby and I wanted to save her life. Now she was of my life.

"And what will happen when they leave all their things here and are gone for so long?" asked Angel. The old ladies had asked him to keep their things and he was worried. "I do not want to keep their belongings in my house. Things will be missing when they get back, and I don't want to be blamed."

No one knew what to do. We had never had strangers living among us and so we had never asked them to leave. And no one of us had ever been so troublesome that we had asked him to leave either. It had never been done in our village, not even in the days of my grand-father's fathers.

"And besides everything else, they are ungrateful. Notzi biris." It was Angel who said it, but everyone agreed.

The next morning, Angel went to the old ladies, carrying the pots they had already stored at his house.

"What is the matter?" Margarita asked him. "We were just bringing you more things to keep for us."

"The village decided it would be better if you don't come back," he said. "We are all very ashamed about the watch. What if it were money? What if it did not reappear? We are too ashamed."

"What?" Margarita looked like she didn't understand. Angel was speaking in Spanish to make sure she understood.

"The village decided it would be better if you don't come back," Angel said again. "We are all very ashamed about the watch. What if it were money? What if it did not reappear? We are too ashamed."

"What?" Margarita still didn't understand.

Angel started to repeat his speech, but Margarita stopped him.

"You don't want us to come back?" she asked.

"Yes. We are too ashamed," said Angel, and went home.

The old ladies sat in their house talking and talking and crying. I watched them from my mother's kitchen. Margarita cried and cried. Joanna kept talking and patting Margarita's shoulder and turning her ring. She looked as scared as the night Margarita had been sick. But this time I didn't know what to do. I wanted to pat Joanna, the way she was patting Margarita, and tell her that it would be all right, the village would not be angry forever. Anger passes. The village was angry at their stinginess. But the village would listen if the old ladies wanted to stay.

The two of them came to my house. Margarita was still crying.

"We are going to go to every house and talk to everyone," Joanna told me. She would talk, I thought. Margarita could only cry and cry. No words were coming out.

"That is good. Tell everyone that you want to stay," I said. "Tell them you like living here. Tell them you want to come back. Tell them you will not be so stingy from now on."

Joanna stared at me. "Yohuashi," she said. Stinginess.

"Yes," I said. "Even babies know it is bad to be stingy."

Joanna nodded. Finally she understood.

"If she doesn't stop crying, that stupid old woman is going to flood the village," my mother said.

I followed them to each house. "We were not at the meeting last night," said Teresa in the house next to mine. "We want you to stay."

No one in the village had been at the meeting, it seemed. Everyone wanted them to come back.

"And you will bring me some green and blue thread, so I can make a beautiful skirt?"

"Of course," they said. "We will bring thread."

"And you will bring those red handkerchiefs you use, like the men who worked rubber in the days of my grandfather?"

"Yes, we will try and find those handkerchiefs."

Angel blew the horn again. This time the old ladies went to the sesión.

"These women should come back to our village," Papaisi said. "They are stingy and they are lazy, but they should come back. They are happy that their watch has reappeared. They give us medicine when we are sick. And they never bother and nag at people to give them meat."

Everyone agreed about that. They didn't beg for meat.

Then Margarita spoke in Spanish. "We chose this village, this Poincushmana, over all the other villages we visited on the whole Paro River. We saw every other village on this river and we asked to live here, here because we thought the people were the nicest of any village. Stealing is not so important. I was very upset about my watch, but I am not so upset anymore. Not about my watch. And not about the beads. I am upset to think that I cannot come back to this village. Please allow us to come back. We want to very much."

I watched Joanna while Margarita spoke. She was nodding and nodding with every word, turning and turning her ring. And with every nod she kept looking at different people, smiling at each one. She looked at me and nodded and nodded. Margarita's voice got stronger as she spoke, and Joanna's nods got bigger. Good. I wanted everyone to listen to them, to understand that they really did want to come back to us, to stay with us longer. And that finally they had begun to know how to live like real people, like us, not like stingy old nawa.

"We will not be stingy anymore," Joanna said. "We have learned from you."

Angel translated Margarita's speech and what Joanna

said, and everyone nodded. "Yes, of course they can come back."

"But I do not want to keep their things in my house," Angel said.

"The old ladies' things should stay at my house. That is the correct place for them." Everyone nodded when Papaisi said this. Yes, that was right. Their things should stay at Papaisi's.

"Good, that is good," said Papaisi. "You will bring me nice thick rubber boots when you return?"

"Yes, of course," said Margarita. "Thank you. And now, it is time for a party."

"About time," my mother said.

Margarita and Joanna went down to the trader's boat and bought three new bottles of sugarcane liquor. Why did they do that? They still had a bottle from their arrival party. They didn't know it was river water. They gave one new bottle to Angel, one to Papaisi, and one to old Bahuin. And the village was happy.

When the three bottles were gone, the old men began asking for the old bottle.

"No," Margarita said gently. "That is for when our house is finished. That bottle is for our new house party."

Good, I thought. It would only make the old ladies

angry when they found out the truth about the bottle. Now everyone was happy. Let it remain so.

Nonti arrived the following day. We all went down to the river to wave good-bye to the old ladies.

"Nora mocai," said the old ladies. We are going.

"Catanhue," the village said. Go and come back.

Nonti started the motor and they went off, chiponqui.

"Good riddance," said my mother. "I hope they don't come back. They are trouble."

"Oh, Mama. They are not that much trouble. They are just different, very different."

"Yes, they are different," she said. "Different from real people. They are nawa, Alicia. Nawa are different. They only like their own kind. They will never like us. That is why I say they are trouble. Because you can never be sure what they are thinking, what they might do. They have no love of us, no appreciation of us. They are nawa. All nawa are the same. They are not the real people. Now go fetch water."

Life was simple for my mother. She knew everything there was to know. Our caibo are good, all others are bad. And that was all there was in the world.

CHAPTER TWELVE   Marco heard the boat first. Marco with his jaguar ears. The boat came up the river about once a year, and there was no mistaking its sound. It was the biggest boat that ever came up our river. It had a real motor, not a pequi-pequi, but a big Evinrude. It would get here soon. It was the only boat that traveled fast. It was the only boat we didn't look forward to seeing. It was the boat the government sent to take young men into the army.

The army took the men to a campamento near Tarapoto, and they made them work the fields that belonged to the army. They fed them only bananas, nothing else. And when they got around to looking at the men, the Isabo men were always too short, or they could not see well enough, or they had something else wrong with them. That was good. At least the men would come back to us. But what was bad was that the army never gave them a paper to say, "You are dismissed from the army. You are not tall enough or you can't hear well enough or whatever the reason would be." No, they just drove the men back up the river and dropped them back in their villages. And the next year they would come and take the same men all over again. So once again they would work the army's fields and eat only bananas. And wait to come home. Why didn't the army look at the men before they took them away? Stupid army.

But mostly, when the boat arrived, there were no young men to be found in the village. We know how to deal with the government. The young men go off into the forest when they hear the boat getting close. And we hide our brothers' clothing. Then we sit and smile at the ugly Peruvian men who come through the village looking for our brothers.

My mother's brother lived a bit upstream from us, at the other end of the village. When my mother heard the boat, she was the first to go to her brother. Her brother's wife had to take care of her own brother. That is the way we are. We girls take care of our brothers.

Let their sisters take care of our husbands. My own brothers were too young to worry about.

I stayed in our house with Cami, watching all the men in the houses near me disappear into the forest. Cami sat propped up in a small wooden box stuffed with old clothes, to help her learn to sit on her own. She was of sitting age now. Elena ran after her brother, bringing him some fariña to take in case the army boat stayed a long time. Canseen ran to get her brother's gun, in case he saw some game while he was hiding.

When the boat docked, there were no young men in the village. The only young man left was Tomas, and he was drunk. He must have hidden a bottle of liquor he received from his patrón and swallowed the whole thing himself. Tomas is Papaisi's only son, and the baby of the family. And what a baby he is. He never does any work for anyone, and his seven older sisters take care of him. This day, Tomas was walking around shouting about the harm someone had done him. Mostly he kept falling down every time he raised his arms to gesture at something he alone saw, something that was disagreeing with him.

As the boat began to dock, Tomas's two youngest sisters yelled at him.

"Get yourself into the forest, you big baby. Do you want to be taken by the government?"

"I cannot be taken," Tomas shouted at something in a tree. "I cannot be taken!"

The two oldest sisters had already hidden all of Tomas's clothes.

"I am a man, I cannot be taken by anyone or anything. I am strong, I am myself. I am owner of myself." After that loud speech Tomas fell to the ground and stayed there.

"Get him out of here, now," Papaisi yelled at his daughters. The two younger daughters pulled Tomas up, put his arms over their shoulders, and dragged him into the forest.

"I am owner of myself!" Tomas yelled. Later, Teolinda told me that she and her sister had stuffed her baby shawl into his mouth to keep him from yelling and then taken him far into the forest, where they tied him to a big tree. Teolinda and her sister went farther into the forest to gather caimito until the army boat left.

The government men came up the riverbank, one big, strong one with a lot of hair and one as small as a boy with no hair on his head. They left another man with a gun in the boat, guarding three Isabos from downriver.

My mother and I sat by our fire, heating up some bananas. My mother's brother was far away, deep in the forest with the other young men. Cami was asleep now in her hammock. She slept like all Isabo baby girls, with her wintoti on her forehead. She smiled in her sleep, a tiny baby smile.

"Hohue," my mother greeted the men.

"Hoho," the big one replied.

"Minqui nocon hande acai?" my mother asked. Did they really speak our language?

"Hoho," the big one said again.

"Good," said my mother. "They only know how to say hello." She reached for her chapo bowl and handed it to the big one. "Bishonhue." Take some.

The man looked at the chapo bowl and gave it back to my mother.

"Who raised that one?" my mother said to me. "He doesn't take the drink I offer him. He is worse than those old ladies. But more dangerous." And my mother smiled at the men.

I kept my head down, stirring the bananas. My mother was having a good time making fun of these men while she pretended to be nice to them. I was not good at that game. I hated these men. They acted as if we were animals, not people, as if they owned us. If I lifted my head so that they could see my face, I would not be able to hide my hatred. I kept my head down.

"Where are the men?" the little one asked in Spanish.

"We ate them all, no more left," my mother answered in Isabo, pretending not to understand Spanish. "We eat only the young ones. Very good and juicy. Once they are old, we don't want them anymore. Too tough. Like alligator skin." All this she said right to their faces.

"Hombres, hombres," the big one said. "Dónde estan?"

My mother rubbed her stomach. "Very tasty they were. That is why all the women are fat. Young men keep us well nourished."

The big one started to get mad. He started to yell, "Dónde estan los hombres del pueblo?"

"If you don't believe me, maybe we should start on you too," my mother kept on. "But you don't look very tasty. No, you are getting too old to be of any use to us. None of us would even have sex with you ugly old roosters."

The men looked disgusted and started walking upriver, toward Papaisi's kitchen.

"Good riddance," my mother yelled after them, waving and smiling at them.

The men waved back at my mother. They had not understood a word she said.

"The ignorant ones are coming to you next," my mother shouted upstream to old lady Yoshran. "Talk to them. They love it when you talk to them." My mother laughed and laughed.

The men stayed in our village until dinnertime, wandering from house to house. They got angrier and angrier. No one offered them food or drink, and finally they went away.

After the boat left, life went on. My father returned from working wood. He brought cloth, some new pots, thread and needles for my mother, and a new shotgun. My mother was very happy.

"I am home for only a short time," my father told us. He patted Cami's head as she slept. "Juan Matus has asked me to return upriver to work wood for him. He says he will pay me very well this time."

"Good," said my mother. "My son brings us fish and little birds. He can provide for us. We will be fine. Go off and earn while you can, before you are too old to work for anyone. We will be fine."

111

My father nodded, and did not mention the stupid old man he said I was promised to.

❦

A few days after my father went reboqui, we heard the sound of Nonti's pequi-pequi and knew the old ladies were coming back. Papaisi blew the horn and got some men working on their house before they arrived. Three days later, there was a real change in it. The roof was begun. The old ladies smiled to see that.

And they brought all the gifts they said they would.

"Angel said there was a plane crash near Sapososta," Papaisi told the old ladies as he held his boots happily. "When I heard about that plane crash, I thought of you. I wondered whether you were on that plane. And I thought a lot about my boots. I wondered if they were on that plane." The old ladies laughed. They seemed happy to be back.

"Where are the pictures?" Elena asked Joanna.

Joanna dug around in one of their boxes and brought out pictures, many, many pictures. These pictures were of us, of our village. The old ladies began to give the pictures to people, to whoever was in them. Joanna gave one to me. I looked at it. It was me, dressed up in my best beads, holding my Cami in her sling, standing next to Elena, whose face was beautifully painted and who was wearing her wonderful tiny-white-bead belt and a new skirt. We looked beautiful, very serious and dressed very well.

"I want one too," Elena said as she looked over my shoulder.

"Of course we have one for you too," said Joanna, and she gave Elena the very same picture.

"So where are your boyfriends?" Elena asked. "Come, let us see the ugly old men."

"We don't have any pictures," said Joanna. "But Margarita has a boyfriend named Flaco and mine is called Dante." Joanna grinned when she told us that.

"What did they give you?" I asked.

"Give us? They didn't give us anything." Joanna looked puzzled. "We went dancing with them in Pucallpa, and we had fun. They didn't give us anything."

"What? What kind of stingy boyfriends did you find?" Elena and I couldn't believe our ears. Even nawa ought to know that boyfriends give you presents. If you are married, of course, they can't give you anything that your husband might discover. But they were not married. Their boyfriends could give them anything.

"Listen," said Elena. "If a woman has sex with a man he should give her something. Sometimes he brings her meat, sometimes he gives her cloth, sometimes thread, needles, whatever. But something, he should give her something. If he gives her nothing, he is a rambi yosi, a bad old man, yoḥuashi, a stingy old man."

"What do your boyfriends give you?" asked Joanna. She was a sly one, that old lady. Just when we were trying to teach her something about how to conduct herself in the world, she started asking more of her questions.

"I have no boyfriends," said Elena. "I am married. But before I was married, I got presents."

"Right, no boyfriends," I said to Elena under my breath. "Your stingy old husband brought you those new yellow beads, right?"

"Before I was married," Elena continued as if I had said nothing, "I received many gifts from boyfriends. Once I even got a flashlight, a Winchester," she said proudly.

"Have you never received presents from boyfriends?" I asked. It was bad enough that they did nothing to make themselves look pretty. But it seemed that they had no self-respect at all.

"We do things differently," said Joanna. "In my country, women are proud to be independent, to be on their own, to depend on no one but themselves. And sex is something you do if and when you want to, for no reward other than the pleasure of doing it."

"Sex without a gift is like roasted plantains without salt," Elena said. "Roasted plantains are good, they will keep you alive, but there is no delight in them. They are just food. But add salt, and they are tasty indeed."

"Even little boys who have sex for the first time bring their little girlfriends gifts, just a little something, some fruit or nuts. It is what sex is about, a trade, a barter, an exchange." I was beginning to sound like Angel the teacher when he taught us about Peru becoming independent from some other government.

"You'll learn, you'll learn," Elena said. "Now tell us all about these stingy old men. Do they dance well? And do they do sex well?" At this we laughed and laughed.

"Yes, they do both well," Margarita said, and we all laughed again. The old ladies were much happier than the first time they came to see us. It felt good to have them back.

CHAPTER THIRTEEN   The rains started. The men could not finish the old ladies' roof in the rain.

All the villages downriver on the Paro flooded every year. The people had to raise their floors and put them higher up in the houses, sometimes way up into the roofs. They would have to live that way, surrounded by water, until the waters went away, living with their chickens and ducks because there was no land in sight. The only way they could get from one house to the next was by canoe. And of course there was nothing to eat, since all the animals ran up into the monte to escape the flooding. At the mouth of the Paro, where it runs into the Ucayali, the flooding was tremendous. In bad years, whole villages had to be abandoned. But our village was never flooded. We lived in a very good spot—high land of the poincus bird. Sometimes the river came all the way up to the top of its bank, but it never flooded. That's why we lived here.

When the rains came, so did the cold. We wrapped up in our shawls and blankets, whatever warm things we had. The old ladies had brought sweaters with them, and they put them on during those rainy days. Margarita had the strangest sweater. It had little spots of color all over it, tiny little spots like gnats. When she first put it on, Elena and I started picking the spots out of it. The sweater looked like it was a nest for many, many tiny colored bugs. Margarita said no, that they were part of the sweater, but we kept picking away. Surely it would look better without all those things on it. But Margarita liked it that way, so we eventually gave in and let her walk around looking like she was wearing something with a disease.

Joanna was sitting under her mosquito net, writing in her notebook and scratching her feet.

"Hohue," I said.

"Hoho," said Joanna. "Why do my feet itch so much? I can hardly do any work because I have to keep scratching my toes and they itch and itch."

"You have been walking barefoot, haven't you?" I

118

asked her. Both of the old ladies had big, thick black boots, perfect to wear in all the mud. But Joanna had stopped wearing them.

"Yes," said Joanna, still scratching her toes. "So what?"

"Now you have worm eggs in your feet. That's why they itch."

Joanna looked terrified. She stopped scratching. "Eggs? Eggs in my feet? Worms put their eggs inside my feet, inside my skin, inside my body?"

I had never seen her act like this before. Usually it was Margarita who yelled and screamed and cried. Joanna was the calm one.

"It's okay," I said. "We all have them. You know how we all have diarrhea and our stomachs hurt us? That's the worms. After they come in through your feet, they crawl up through your legs and into your stomach and make you feel sick."

Joanna stared at me. "Worms put eggs in my feet? Really? There are eggs in my feet right now? Are there worms in there too?" She began turning her ring.

"No. The worms live in the mud. When the ground is wet and there is mud, that's when the worms live there. And that's when they lay their eggs in your feet.

When the eggs hatch, your feet won't itch anymore." I thought that might cheer her up, but she looked even more upset.

"When my feet don't itch, then the eggs have hatched and then I have no more eggs in my feet, but soon I will have worms in my stomach?"

She did understand, and she was not happy about it.

"Yes. That's right. Now the thing to do is to put heat on your toes, where they itch the most. Heat up anything and put it on your toes. It will stop the itch for a while."

"How big are the worms when they get to my stomach? Can you see them travel up your legs when they hatch?" Joanna was staring at her toes.

"Sometimes they get big, like a snake," I said, "but mostly they are little. Like regular worms. But you have medicine for them. You brought us medicine, so I know you have the medicine. You can take it and kill the worms."

"The worm medicine we brought," Joanna said.

"Right. I just didn't know that they got into your stomach through your feet and that they itch so terribly." She had recovered enough to begin her scratching again. "Between the lice in my hair and the worm eggs in my feet, I spend more time scratching than working."

It still sounded strange to me that she called what she did "working." When an Isabo man says he is working, he is clearing a garden, going out hunting, building a house, weaving a sleeping mat, making a canoe, chopping and carrying home firewood. When an Isabo woman says she is working, she is planting a garden, harvesting food from the garden, gathering wild fruits and nuts, making a fire, cooking food, spinning cloth, weaving cloth, making pottery. And when these old ladies said they were working, they were asking us questions and writing in their notebooks. Then they would read some books, talk some more, write some more, ask more questions, and write again.

"Where is Cami?" Joanna asked, as she continued to scratch her toes.

"My mother took her to Weesoshando to visit her brother's wife today. They'll be home by nightfall."

"Someday I'd like to go to Weesoshando," Joanna said. "I've heard so much about it."

Weesoshando is an Isabo village two turns of the river downstream from us.

"We'll go soon," I told her. "There are a lot of papaya trees right near Weesoshando, and the papayas will be getting ripe soon. We will go one day and get papayas and visit Weesoshando."

"Good. Maybe by then I won't be itching so much."

That afternoon the rain stopped for a while and Papaisi stood in the middle of the road and blew his horn. He blew the horn a number of times, went back in his house to put the horn away, picked up his machete, and went to work on the old ladies' house. Other men came with their machetes. Joanna and Margarita came out to watch.

"We will have this house finished in three days," Papaisi said proudly.

"That would be good," said Margarita. "But it looks like it will take more work than that."

"Three days," said Papaisi. "We are strong, we are hard workers. Three days."

"Okay," said Margarita.

"The men could use some oatmeal soup to help them work," said Papaisi.

"We'll make some now," said Margarita. The old ladies made it thick, so you almost had to chew it. We make it more like chapo, like a drink.

When the old ladies came back with the oatmeal, Papaisi handed it out to all the men who were working. Then he sat down next to Joanna and started telling her what a wonderful, hardworking village we were. Joanna nodded and nodded. Then Papaisi said, "We will put a floor in only half of the house. We will leave the other half without a floor. For dancing," he said, and smiled at the old ladies.

"No," said Margarita. "We want the floor for the whole house. We can dance somewhere else."

Papaisi drank his oatmeal. "See how nice the house would look with only half a floor," he said.

"No," said Margarita. "We want a floor for the whole house."

Papaisi drank some more oatmeal and said, "Fine. But then the house will take longer than three days."

"Fine," said Margarita. "But we want a floor for the whole house."

"The whole house," said Papaisi.

"And we will wait," said Margarita.

"And you will wait," said Papaisi.

My mother returned from Weesoshando that afternoon and handed me the baby.

"She is a good girl. She sat by herself for a long time at my brother's wife's house. She was proud of herself, proud of learning to sit up. And watch her hands. She will be a good fisher. See how she is practicing taking the fish off the hook." We both watched as my little

Cami pulled one finger on her left hand with her right hand.

"See! She does it over and over." My mother had never said a good word about this baby since I had taken her. But now she seemed to think she was going to live, at least long enough to go fishing. I hoped she was right.

Elena came by later and we sat at my mother's hearth, drawing designs in the dirt. Joanna and Margarita stopped by on their way to bathe.

"What are you two gossiping about?" Joanna asked. Elena had just taught them the Isabo word for gossip.

"Marriage, husbands, whatever it would be," Elena giggled.

"Oh," said Joanna.

"Did you really never have a husband?" I asked Joanna.

"Really," she said. "Never. Margarita did. A really bad old one. But not anymore. She got rid of him."

"Why did you throw him away?" I asked Margarita.

"He was mean to me," Margarita said. "And I stopped loving him when he was mean to me."

"Didn't you have any boyfriends who were nice to you?" I asked. Who cares if your husband is not nice?

Husbands are not supposed to be nice. They are supposed to clear your gardens and bring home meat.

"I didn't have any boyfriends until I left my husband," said Margarita. "That's the way we do it."

"You were married to a man you didn't like and you didn't have any boyfriends?"

"Yes," she said.

The rains started again. Joanna and Margarita had missed their baths, but they didn't seem to mind. They did love to talk, those two. The rainy season would be a great time for them. When it's cold and rainy, no one does very much outside the house. People stay at home—even the men—and try to stay warm.

"And your husband," Joanna said to me. "I hear he is coming back."

"He's not my husband," I said.

"Are you happy that he is coming back?" She did not understand.

"Happy or whatever I would be," I said.

"Will he be happy to have another baby?" Joanna asked.

"He has no baby," I said. Did she think I was pregnant?

"Cami," Joanna said.

"That is not his baby," I told her. "That is my baby. I adopted her. That old man has nothing to do with her."

"But he is your husband," Joanna said.

"Only my father says so," I said. "But even if he were my husband, the baby is my baby. My adopted baby. Not my husband's baby. Mine."

Joanna and Margarita looked puzzled.

"My beads are my beads," I said. "My skirts are my skirts. This baby is my baby. He did not help to create her." What was so hard to understand?

CHAPTER FOURTEEN Each day now, when the rains stopped, Papaisi blew his horn and the men worked on the old ladies' house. And every time they heard the horn, one of the old ladies would boil up a big pot of oatmeal for the men, without anyone asking them. Slowly, over the next few weeks, the work was finished. The house was big and strong, and it had flooring from one side to the other.

"It is done," Papaisi announced to the old ladies. And the three of them went to examine the house.

"It is good, a good house," Papaisi said. "Just like we promised you."

The old ladies were happy. "Thank you," they said. "It is beautiful."

"So now we will have a real party to welcome you to your new house," said Papaisi.

"Yes," they agreed. "Tonight we will have a party."

We all helped them carry their things from Chawa's house into their new house. First they strung up their enormous mosquito net and then they arranged everything inside it. They had much more space than they did at Chawa's, and they kept moving things around until they were just as they wanted them.

It was time to eat, but they had no kitchen. The men had spent their time building the house. Cuncha had taken some firewood from her mother's hearth and started a fire for the old ladies—a fire out in the open, like you make when you are on a hunting trip.

Margarita went to Papaisi's house.

"We love our house," she said. "And now we need a kitchen."

"Of course you do," said Papaisi. "We will build it tomorrow. After the party, you will have your kitchen. It will only take us a day to build a kitchen."

That night, the old ladies got out their old bottle of liquor and some cups. Everyone gathered at their house. The old ladies were smiling and laughing. What would they do when they discovered the truth?

"Hacon shobo," Joanna said. What a good house.

"This thatch we got for you will last forever. No rain will come through your roof. You will always be dry in this house. The men built it with great care and attention, and they searched the forest far, far away for the best materials to use." Papaisi made his speech and sat down on their new flooring.

"And the floors are strong, strong and good. They will last forever too. The wood for the floors comes from deep in the forest, two days' walk from here. We built you a wonderful house."

"Yes," said Margarita. "You built us a wonderful house." And she said no more.

These women had learned how to talk to the elders. It had taken them a long time, but they finally did learn.

By now everyone was sitting on the floor of their house or on the ground, swatting the mosquitoes away. Joanna started passing out cups of the liquor to the old men first. She gave the first cup to Papaisi. He took a sip.

"This is not liquor. This is river water," he announced, and spit the liquid on the ground.

Joanna and Margarita looked at each other. We all waited.

"They came from Weesoshando and stole your liquor," said someone softly.

"However it would be," said Margarita with a smile.

"Whoever it would be," said Joanna.

What had happened to these old ladies?

"We'll play our music," said Joanna. "That will be our party for our new house." She brought out their tape recorder and turned it on.

"What does it say?" I asked.

"It is a song about a box of rain," said Joanna, with tears in her eyes. "Just a box of rain, I don't know who put it there," she sang.

"More silliness," my mother said. "Boxes filled with rain. The water would run through a box. They should sing about tins of rain, buckets of rain, pails of rain, gasoline containers of rain. Nawa."

We all laughed at my mother. Joanna played the song again. And we all sang, "Such a long long time to be gone and a short time to be there."

The old ladies didn't care that someone had taken something of theirs! Maybe because they didn't like sugarcane liquor, maybe they were just so happy to finally have their house that nothing else mattered to them, or maybe they were learning how to be. Whatever reason it would be.

⟡

The next morning, the men dragged some posts and some thatch over to the old ladies' house and put up a little kitchen for them, just a thatched roof. That is all our kitchens are, no floor, of course, since your fire has to be on the ground. They built a small kitchen, big enough for only two people. Margarita was off doing her work in someone's garden when the men were building the kitchen. She came back in the evening.

"Look. How quickly they built our kitchen!" Joanna was happy. Cuncha was happy. And a wonderful stew was cooking on the fire. I was sitting with Cuncha at the fire. I sat Cami right next to me. She could sit by herself, but she still toppled over sometimes.

"Why did they build it here?" asked Margarita.

"What? What do you mean? They built it here because you always build a kitchen across from your house, nearer to the river. All the kitchens are built this way. What are you talking about?"

"Get up. Stand back here. This kitchen is not in the line of the kitchens. It is too close to the house. All the other kitchens are in one line, one straight line all down the village. The same distance away from the line of houses. Our house is in the right line. But our kitchen sticks out of the line. Don't you see?"

Joanna, Cuncha, and I all looked. Margarita was right. It did look funny.

"You are turning into a good Isabo," I told Margarita.

"You are getting a sense of design and symmetry from living with us."

"Yes," said Margarita. "And I want them to move the kitchen."

Symmetry and design are one thing. Moving a kitchen is another. "Go tell Papaisi," I said to her.

"Yes," she said. "I will do that. But not today. Today we will just be happy to have a kitchen, even if it is in the wrong place."

The next day I went with Margarita to tell Papaisi that the kitchen should be moved.

"Yes, all in good time," he answered. "After the rainy season. No work can be done now until the rains stop."

Margarita nodded and went back to her house.

"Enough is never enough with them," Papaisi said, laughing. "They always want more, always something more than they have. It's a difficult way to be."

"They are different," I said. "But they are learning."

The rains came and went, came and went. It wasn't a bad rainy season for us, although many villages down-river were flooded. One morning before the rain began,

132

Papaisı blew the horn and the men moved the old ladies' kitchen.

Later that morning, Marco perked up his little jaguar ears.

"Avión," he whispered. "An airplane is coming."

Soon the rest of us heard it too. We all ran down to the river to watch the plane land on its skis on the river, like a big chara bird. We knew it was gringo missionaries. They always fly the same dark green planes. Joanna and Margarita had come down to the river to watch too.

"Who is it?" Joanna asked me, turning her ring.

"Your kinsmen," I told her. "American missionaries."

The missionaries got out of the plane. Two were old ladies, like Joanna and Margarita, but they wore dresses with little flowers all over them and sandals with high heels. Their skin was the color of a paiché fish's belly, and their hair was the color of Margarita's, but it was all twisty, like a very old river. Their voices sounded like the squawks of tete birds. They were fat, but that was the only beautiful thing about them.

The man who drove the plane went right up to Joanna and put out his hand. They both smiled and talked a bit. Then the man said something to her. Whatever it was, it made Joanna really mad. *Really* mad. The man kept smiling, but Joanna didn't.

Margarita was shaking the hand of each of the old lady missionaries. They talked and talked at Margarita while the man showed Joanna the plane he had driven. Then all of them stood around in a big group and talked in their language. We all stood back and watched. No one sat down. They just stood there in the middle of the path and talked and talked.

Finally Angel came out to greet them and invite them to stay in his house. The two lady missionaries told the man to carry their stuff—boxes and boxes of stuff—into Angel's house.

"What did that old man say to you that made you so mad?" I asked Joanna when the missionaries had gone into Angel's house and Joanna and Margarita were left standing alone.

"He asked me if the women here take care of their children," Joanna said. "What is wrong with these people? Can't they see with their own eyes? Of course the mothers here take care of their children. Can't they just look at the children? The children are all cared for, all beautiful, sweet children. These people are crazy, tsindi biris."

"They are your people," I said. "Aren't they? They speak your language, don't they?"

"Yes," said Joanna. "We speak the same language, but they are not my people. Their beliefs are not my beliefs. They are not like us at all. Look at all the stuff they brought. They are only staying for one night and they brought more than we brought for months!"

They *had* brought a lot of stuff. Most of it was food —bacon, a cake called Betty something, bags and bags of candy, mattresses to sleep on, and bread. Joanna and Margarita had brought lots of stuff—much more than we had ever seen before—but these women brought things that even Joanna and Margarita hadn't seen before, at least not here, in the jungle.

Joanna, Margarita, Elena, and I waited until the missionaries got settled in Angel's house and then went over to visit.

"They better give us some of that candy," said Joanna. "They brought so much. And one of those bags is filled with white chocolate candy bars. Big, thick chocolate candy bars. They better offer us some."

Joanna and Margarita sat on Angel's porch, chatting with the missionary ladies. We sat on the ground nearby. As they talked, the missionary ladies kept eating the

135

cooked bacon they had brought. Joanna's eyes never left the plate of bacon, and the missionary ladies didn't offer her any. They just kept talking and eating. Joanna was almost drooling.

"So *all* of your people are stingy," I whispered to Joanna.

She took her eyes off the bacon and looked at me.

"It seems so, doesn't it?" Joanna whispered back.

Then one of the missionaries went looking through one of their boxes and brought out a big bag of chocolate. Each missionary lady took a bar and then they put the bag back in the box. I thought Joanna was going to grab the bag out of the box and run. But she just kept chatting calmly, although her eyes never left the box that the bag of candy was in. Her hands were busy turning her ring. Finally, one of the missionaries reached for the bag again——those women ate constantly——and she finally noticed that Joanna kept staring at the chocolate. She gave Joanna and Margarita each a chocolate bar and ate a few more bars herself.

Joanna and Margarita unwrapped their candy, each took a tiny piece, and Joanna gave me hers and Margarita gave hers to Elena to divide up among all of us who were watching.

"Yohuashi biris," said Joanna to me, indicating the

missionary ladies. "They have so much chocolate, and they are so stingy with it."

Joanna looked at me and then looked at everyone sharing that one bar of chocolate, and something happened to her. I could almost see the thought go through her body—the way she was being with the missionaries was the way we had been with her, wanting everything they had and not understanding why they were so stingy. I just nodded at her.

Later that evening, when it was dark, the missionaries called a meeting of the village to tell us, in Spanish, that we should not do our pui in the river anymore, but should dig holes in the jungle and make pui there. Angel translated. Nobody laughed out loud, because we didn't want to insult the missionaries, but no one could believe what they were telling us.

"Make pui in a big hole in the jungle?" asked Nimeran. "They did that in Moshi a few years ago. My brother told me about it. The hole gets filled up with pui—very smelly—and filled with the worms they keep telling us they don't want us to get. And then do you know what comes to those big holes to eat? Snakes! All kinds of snakes. Imagine. We spend hours clearing out all the growth around our houses to keep snakes away from the village, and they come along and tell us to build pui holes to attract them! These people are crazy!"

Everyone giggled, as quietly as we could. Angel was supposed to translate what everyone was talking about.

"The village has no shovels to dig such a hole," said Angel with a straight face. "But we will dig one with our machetes. It may take some time, but we will do it. We want to improve ourselves."

The missionaries smiled and clapped their hands together.

"But we don't want to die!" Nimeran said. "Imagine, sitting down to make pui and getting bit by a hergon. You would die before your pui hit the bottom of the hole." He loved to go on and on, especially when Angel couldn't translate what he was saying.

"Nimeran says he will begin in the morning," Angel told the missionaries.

They smiled and clapped again.

"The village thanks you," said Angel. "Please come back to our village again soon. But not too soon," he added in Isabo.

❦

The same night, a regatón docked just downstream of my house. He had a lot of liquor. Joanna and Margarita went down with us. They had spent the evening talking to the missionaries and watching them eat. By the time the trader docked, they were ready for something different. They bought a big bottle of liquor and passed it around. And they both started to get drunk, really drunk. Icha palna. Their first time.

"Do you think they will be all right?" Elena whispered to me.

Joanna started to sing some of her songs in her own language. Margarita just sat there giggling to herself. Every so often the two of them would look at each other and laugh. They kept putting their fingers to their lips and making "shh, shh" sounds, and then they'd laugh some more.

"Shh, shh," Joanna kept saying. "Don't want to wake the missionaries."

"Right. Nimeran hasn't dug their pui hole yet. They may have to do their business in the river, like the rest of us," said Margarita.

"Too bad. Maybe we should dig a hole just for them. And put a hergon in it." Joanna laughed at her own joke. "Do you play that?" she asked the trader, pointing to his guitar standing in the corner.

"A little bit. Can you play?"

"Yes." Joanna took the guitar and started strumming

She hummed and strummed, and Margarita laughed. Then she started playing some song, bouncing up and down and singing loud.

"Shh, shh," Margarita kept telling her.

Joanna started to sing softly, but then she got louder again. She played and sang and played and sang. The more we drank, the better the music sounded. Finally she started to sing the banana song.

"Shboom, shboom," she kept singing, louder and louder. We all sang with her.

Angel arrived and told us that the missionaries had finally gone to sleep. They had stayed up and told Angel how happy they were that the village was going to dig their pui holes and how much better the village would feel and how much better it would be for Joanna and Margarita to be living in a village with "latrines."

Joanna and Margarita laughed and talked and laughed and talked and kept drinking. They hugged each other and hugged me and passed around the bottle to everyone. They only spoke in Isabo and Spanish that night.

"I think we are both a little homesick," Joanna said finally, turning her ring. "Non caibo shinandai."

"So now you have your wish. You have people from your country visiting you here," Angel said. And we all laughed until we cried.

"People from my country," said Joanna. "But not my people. Not my caibo."

"You know what I want when you go back to your country?" Nimeran asked. Nimeran was as drunk as everyone else. "You know what I want?"

"Yes. You want us to bring you big rubber boots like Papaisi's," said Joanna.

"No, he wants good hunting dogs. About four of them," said Angel.

"No. He wants you to bring him a new ax," said Shori.

"No," said Elena. "He wants a watch and a big bolt of red cloth."

"You are all wrong," said Nimeran. "This is what I want. I want you to take me with you. I want to see your land. I want to see what a real city is like. I want to see your rivers and your gardens. I want to eat food I have never seen before. I want to see everything before I die. Everything. Take me with you, please."

Joanna and Margarita both stared at him. Neither one of them could speak. A tear dripped down Joanna's cheek. And then Nimeran passed out.

We all laughed. Old Nimeran. Who would have known he had such dreams?

CHAPTER FIFTEEN My little Cami was sick. She started to have diarrhea in the morning. I gave her to my mother to nurse.

"She's not sucking very hard," my mother said. "She looks weak and she feels cold. We will drip my breast milk into her mouth. Go ask the old ladies for some rice to feed her."

My mother started to drip the milk from her breasts into Cami's mouth. She held her mouth open and then closed it for her. The baby was very weak. I went and asked the old ladies for some rice. Joanna gave it to me and said, "Is there anything else I can give you? Is there any of our medicine that would help? Can Papaisi cure her?"

"No, my mother is caring for her." I started to leave,

and Joanna asked if I wanted some sugar to go with the rice.

"Sugar will help her," she said, but I thought she didn't believe it.

I took some sugar and went back home.

"She is vomiting now too. She has the vomiting and diarrhea sickness. She will not live very long."

I knew my mother was right. She had been through this with her own children and with the children of others. She had seen many children die. My mother's healthy, fat, one-year-old daughter, Pena, had died in less than a day from the vomiting and diarrhea sickness. Even her fat could not stop death. My little Cami could be taken much more quickly.

I boiled up the rice, added some sugar to it, and chewed it until it was as thin as my mother's milk. I took the baby from my mother and squeezed the rice milk into her mouth, a very little at a time. I rubbed her throat to try and make her swallow.

"Please drink, please drink," I sang softly to her. "Only if you drink can you grow healthy and strong. Please drink."

My mother went off to get bananas from her garden. I sat by myself in the house, trying to feed this baby who did not want to be fed. She just wanted to be left alone. She was too tired to swallow. I kept dripping rice milk into her mouth anyway; I kept rubbing her throat to make her swallow. I held her in my lap and dripped and rubbed. Next to me I kept a skirt I was working on so I could pick it up and embroider whenever anyone walked by. I didn't want to talk about my baby. I didn't want to hear what anyone had to say about her.

Nachi stopped by on her way to her garden.

"Chishotai?" she asked. Diarrhea?

"Yes," I said.

"Queenandai?" Is she throwing up too?

I nodded yes.

"Mahuacasai." She wants to die.

"Yes," I said. "She wants to die."

"Era mocai." I am going now.

"Catanhue," I said. Go and come back.

Nachi was the only one I wanted to see. Everyone else had thought I was crazy to take this baby, crazy to feed this baby, crazy to care for this baby. No one would wail when she died; no one but me would care at all that she was gone.

When Nachi left, I wanted to be alone. There was an empty Sanitario Post where the medicines from the government were kept when we had medicines in the village. Now it was empty. The Sanitario Post had walls. That was what I wanted. Walls around me. I did not want everyone to come by and see me crying over my dying nawa. Everyone would know, but they didn't have to see.

My baby died on the walk to the post. I felt her die; she just wasn't breathing anymore. She was gone. I sat inside the Sanitario Post and held her, my head bent over her, all wrapped up in my shawl. My tears fell on her cold little body. The tears just sat there. I wiped them off and more fell. It was bad enough that she was dead, I didn't have to make her all wet too.

I sat there crying over my dead baby. A few people came by, saw me, and left. I didn't look up to greet them. Finally Joanna came over.

"I am so sorry," she said. "So sorry."

She patted me on the head, then she patted the dead baby's head. I moved aside so that she could step up into the house and sit with me.

"Yacahue," I told her. Sit down.

She sat down behind me and rubbed my back, slowly. It felt wonderful. My head was hanging over the dead baby to hide my tears, and my back and neck hurt. We sat in silence for the longest time. A few others came by but no one stayed. After a few people came and went, Joanna started to stand up.

"Minqui cai?" Now you are going?

Joanna sat down and looked at me. There were tears in her eyes. She looked confused for a minute, like she wasn't sure how to behave. I kept looking at her and finally she said, "No. Era cayamai." No, I'm not going.

I hung my head down again, and she rubbed my back. We stayed there like that until Nachi came with a funeral urn, a wide urn with no neck, to bury my baby in. Nachi put the urn down next to me and said, "It's time. Let's go bury her. Juan will take us upstream."

Juan was another one of Nachi's adopted children. Juan had a mother and a father, but Nachi had taken him at an early age and Juan still treated her like his mother.

Joanna started to leave again, and I asked her to come to the burial with us.

"Yes," she said. "I will come."

She seemed so unlike Joanna. She wasn't sure what to do, to sit or stand, to leave or stay. This Joanna did what she was told, and if no one told her anything, she just looked awkward and out of place. Maybe it was death that made her that way.

On the way upstream, our canoe passed Nimeran alone in his canoe, coming downstream. He looked at us, and then at me.

"Min baque mahuata?" he asked. Your baby died?

"Nocon baque mahuata," I said. My baby is dead.

Not many people called this nawa my baby. I was glad it was Nimeran we passed on the way to the burial ground. Nimeran knew how much I cared about Cami, and he didn't care that she was a nawa.

When we got to the burial ground, Nachi took the urn out of the canoe, and Juan went to dig a hole in the jungle. Joanna stayed right next to me. We waited for Juan to finish. I wrapped my baby in her worn little shawl and put her wintoti on her forehead. Then I put her inside the urn. Nachi patted her head and put the urn in the hole, and Juan covered it with the earth he had dug. Joanna's eyes were full of tears, and she kept wiping them as they dripped down. I patted her back.

"Icha shipinshona riqui," Nachi said, pointing to some fruit a little downstream. We all trooped over to gather branches of these sweet little pods. Then Juan climbed a papaya tree and threw down a lot of ripe papayas. It was a good day for a burial. There was much ripe fruit to be gathered.

Joanna went to her house as soon as we got back to the village. Margarita was still not back from measuring the gardens, and I saw Joanna get inside her mosquito net and lie down. I thought she might still be crying, but I wasn't sure. I think she went to sleep. Nachi and Juan helped carry all the fruit up to our houses. I gave Juan some of my papayas for helping me. He is my mother's brother's son, but he helped because of Nachi, his mother's sister, his adoptive mother.

The rest of the day my arm kept reaching for Cami on my hip, then it fell uselessly at my side. My mother said nothing, but she didn't order me around for the whole day. When Pena died, we killed her little puppy. Because its owner had died. My Cami had no puppy. There was nothing else to be done.

I didn't see Joanna for the rest of the day. I think she stayed in her mosquito net and didn't come out at all. The next morning Margarita came over and said that she was sorry about Cami. I nodded, and didn't say anything. There was nothing to say. When people die, they die. And then they are no more. The rest who are alive go on living. What is to say? But Margarita seemed to want to say something. She said she was sorry again, and that it must feel bad. I nodded and kept on with my spinning. Was she trying to make me cry? What was she talking about that baby for? It was all over. We had buried her. She was no more. When it is one of our caibo that we bury, we get drunk and wail and carry on, but even with our caibo, once the burial is over, it is over.

"Among Joanna's caibo," Margarita was saying, "their people mourn for a week, seven whole days. They sit in their houses and eat and cry and in the days of their ancestors, they ripped their clothes. Joanna always gets upset when she witnesses death."

I nodded. "We do not mourn for seven days," I said. "We just mourn until the burial. Then we speak no more of the death." I hoped that would make Margarita stop talking about my baby. If that didn't work, I would get up and go gathering.

"Among my people," Margarita went on, "we mourn for only one day. We all get drunk and sit in a room with the body and talk about the person and get more and more drunk and then the next day we bury them." That was a little closer to what I knew, but I still wanted her to stop talking.

"I am going gathering," I said, standing up and putting my spinning away. Margarita looked startled. "I am going," I said, and I picked up my basket and started off toward the jungle.

Later, after I returned from gathering, I was helping my mother make pots. Joanna came over. Her eyes were red. It was the day after the burial and she was still crying. I knew she would begin to speak of Cami.

"I am sorry," she said. "I still feel so bad. You tried so hard to keep Cami alive, and you were doing such a good job. She was doing so well and then, so suddenly, she was gone."

"Yes. Margarita told me you get upset when you witness death." I knew the only way to keep her from talking about Cami was to get her talking about herself, about her own loss.

"Yes." The tears came to her eyes again. "I was only six when my mother died. That was the hardest year of my life."

"Your mother is dead," my mother said to Joanna.

"Yes," Joanna said.

"You are just like me," said my mother. "My mother is dead. My father is dead. I am all alone."

"Now she is not so different, Mama? Now that you are both orphans?"

My mother kept rolling the long coils of clay into bowls.

"All alone," said my mother. "Who adopted you?

Who raised you? Your mother's brother?"

"No," said Joanna. "We don't have that custom, like you do. I still lived with my father, in his house. He went to work every day, I went to school. My mother's friends, the mothers of my friends, they were the ones who took care of me. I went to their houses to eat, they took me shopping to buy clothes. They were my onan titas. Two of them—Ruth and Esther. I called them my aunts, my watas, but they weren't really my watas. They were just friends. My best friends' mothers."

"And your father's new wife? She didn't take care of you?"

"My father didn't have a new wife. He never took another wife. Never. He died without another wife."

"Rambi yosi," said my mother. "What a bad old man. So these women had to take care of him too?"

"Yes, they did. I never thought of it that way, but yes, they took care of him. They adopted both of us."

"Rambi yosi," my mother repeated. "Hahuen baqui shincashamai." The bad old man never thought of his child.

CHAPTER SIXTEEN   That afternoon I went to the river to bathe with Joanna and Margarita. The river was very high, and we had to hang on to the branches that grew out of the riverbanks if we did not want to be carried downstream. I love the river when it is that way—so full and strong. We splashed and swam around and then put shampoo in our hair and soap on our bodies.

When we came back, Olivia, Elena's little sister, was leaning up against my mother's house, waiting for us. She had brought Joanna a pisha her mother had made, to trade for some rice. Margarita went to get the rice, and Olivia said to Joanna, "Joanna, what color is my dress?"

"It's blue, Olivia. Blue like the sky."

Olivia looked Joanna straight in the eye and said, "No, Joanna, it is yellow, yellow like a paoti."

"No," Joanna said, "your dress is blue. Just look at it."

"Yellow." Olivia said. "Pure yellow."

This went on for a while, until Joanna looked at me and said, "I am almost beginning to believe that her dress is yellow, even though it is as blue as it has ever been."

Olivia did not take her eyes from Joanna's eyes.

Margarita returned with the rice, gave it to Olivia, and Olivia ran home.

"Why did she do that? Why did she keep telling me her dress was yellow when we could all see that it was blue?" Joanna asked me.

"Whyever it would be," I said.

"In my country," Joanna said, "children do that kind of thing as a game, to try and fool grown-ups. You tell the grown-up that you already took a bath, when the dirt from the playground is still all over you. And the grown-ups laugh and make you take a bath."

Margarita looked at Joanna, who explained, in their language, what had just happened with Olivia.

"But Olivia was very serious about this game," Joanna said.

"Of course," I said. "Learning to lie well is a serious matter. That is something that all children must practice to learn well."

"Yes," said Joanna. "That's it. She was practicing lying. Lying when all could see that it was a lie."

"Everyone knows when a lie is a lie," I said. "Who cares about that?"

"Really?" Joanna asked.

Margarita was shocked. "In our country, no one is supposed to know you are telling a lie. It is bad to tell a lie. Very bad. And it is very, very bad to have someone know you are lying."

"Why is it bad? Is it better to just say to your own kinsman, 'No, you cannot have any of my food'? That is no way to behave to your own people. That is hurtful and mean. Your kinsman feels angry and ashamed and uncared for. No. The proper thing is to lie. 'I have no food, my dear mother's brother,' or whatever he is to you. Then he may still be hungry, but he is not hurt and without family."

Joanna stared at me. "You are becoming an anthropologist yourself," she said.

"Anthropologist or whatever it would be," I said. I picked up a piece of straw and began drawing a design in the dirt.

"You make beautiful designs," Margarita said. "Isabo designs are the best in the whole forest."

"Of course," I said. "But some women are better than others. Nachi makes the most beautiful designs in the village. Teresa makes the best pots, but her designs are not as good as Nachi's. And the best weaver is Yaya."

"Do your mothers sit down and teach you how to do these things?" Joanna asked.

"No, but we sit with our mothers all day long and watch them, and when we are old enough, our mothers let us have our own piece of clay and we try to make our own little pots. That is how we learn. But the designs come from our heads. The designs we make up. Some like to do it and others don't. I like to do it, but I am not very good yet. I need more years to learn."

"In my country," Joanna said, "we don't learn that many things from our mothers. We learn to cook and things like that, but the work we do, we learn at school. So different. My mother didn't work. She stayed home and took care of me until she died."

156

They were so strange. They called talking to people and writing things down work, and then said that everything her mother did was not work.

"Do you miss your mother?" I asked.

"Miss her or whatever," Joanna said.

CHAPTER SEVENTEEN   The old ladies went to Pucallpa once more and came back once more. The next
time, they would leave for good, they would go back
to their country. And Nonti was not going to pick them
up. This time, they would fly away in an airplane.

"What will you do when you go back to your country?" my mother asked Joanna. "Will you be as lazy
there as you are here? Here you do no real work. You
just sit and talk and sit and write. Is that what you will
do when you go back to your home?"

Joanna came to be with us every morning now. She
always brought coffee to share with me and my mother.
And my mother had begun to talk to her.

"Chiquishashamai." I am not lazy. "I will start to

159

write my thesis, my book, about what I have learned from living with you," she said.

"Write or whatever. That can't take up all your time. You write here, and look how much time you have to bother us with all your questions. Take all your question time and do push-push with some healthy men. Find good men, strong men, men who can make a baby, not the men you have been giving it to," my mother said as she stirred up the fire and put some bananas on to roast. "It is time to make babies. You are old. Soon you will be dead. Then it will be too late to make babies. No good man wants to have sex with an old dead one."

"But I must write my book," said Joanna. "That must come first. Then babies."

"So write the book. What's so hard? You just sit and write here all day. Lazy people's work. It's not so much work to make a baby, you lazy old thing. More fun to make the baby," my mother giggled. "Write and do push-push. It will help you write. You probably don't do enough push-push to make a baby. That's the problem." My mother had spoken. She picked up her basket. "I am going to gather shipinshona," and she walked off reboqui.

"She is going to meet old man Chichica," I whispered to Joanna.

Joanna stared at me.

"She is going to meet old man Chichica in the woods, to have sex." Sometimes, even after all this time, I had to explain every little thing.

"Your mother?" she whispered. "Is going to have sex in the woods with old man Chichica?"

"Yes. They have been doing it for years." I stirred the pot of deer stew my mother had bubbling on the fire and turned over the bananas that were roasting in the embers.

"There goes old lady Yoshran," I said. "See. She is going into the woods from here. She is having sex with Papaisi. Soon Yoshran will come out of the woods further reboqui and Papaisi will come out of the woods chiponqui. They do that so no one will know, but we all know. Everyone knows. There are no secrets here." I pulled the basket with my embroidery in it down from the rafters. Joanna just sat there, her coffee getting cold in the cup.

"What's the matter?" I asked her. "Don't people have sex in your country?"

By the time Papaisi came back from having sex with Yoshran, I had gone home with Joanna. He came to the old ladies' house.

"I will be so sad when you leave," Papaisi began. "I will be happy sitting in my big mosquito net that you are giving me, but I will be sad thinking of you, so far away, in your country."

"We will miss you too," Joanna said. "But we are happy to give you our big mosquito net, for all your kindness to us." Joanna was doing very well. She understood Papaisi's request and promised it to him right away.

"We will have parties in your house when you are gone," he continued. "Parties to remember you and think of you. We will take the floor out of the house. My house needs a new floor. I will put your floor in my house and we will dance in your house. Everyone will be happy and remember you."

After a few minutes Papaisi left. "Will our house stay here for parties?" Joanna asked me.

"No. It will be used by those who need it. Papaisi will take the floor. Ashandi will take the thatch to patch his roof. And Eosario will use your kitchen to make his bigger. Your house will not go to waste," I said.

"Good," said Joanna. "Good."

I felt sad to see them go and never come back. The old ladies had learned enough to become caibo, caibo raibirai. Real people, kinsmen, or whatever they would be.

"Who do you think we should give our good boots to?" Joanna asked me.

"Whoever it would be," I said. I didn't want to be a part of this. I was not the owner of any of their things. They owned them, and they should give them away. But I did want one of the soft, silky bags they slept in.

"Who will you give that bag to?" I pointed. Joanna looked at me. They had been here a year. They should understand what I meant. They should understand that if I asked about it, I wanted it.

"I think we should give it to you," Joanna said. "I think you should have my sleeping bag and Elena should have Margarita's. What do you think?"

"Whatever it would be," I said, and went home.

The old ladies spent the next few days making lists and chattering to each other and making new lists. They were still deciding which of their things to give away. They had the good sense to talk about their things in their own language. They weren't going to give their things away until the day they left. So it was good that they didn't say who got what. It would be too long to wait for your gift. Of course we were all talking about the same thing the old ladies were.

163

"Do you suppose Papaisi will get that big old mosquito net?" my mother asked her sister Nachi.

"He is the only fool who would want it," Nachi said. "It's too big to be of any use. Too many mosquitoes get into it all day long. You have to kill them at night before you go to sleep. Useless." Nachi thought for a moment. "Papaisi would like it. It looks like something only a headman should have. Arrogant old man." My mother and Nachi laughed and laughed.

"What I want," Teolinda said, "is their big pot. Mine is old and wearing thin. I need a new one, and my husband would rather buy sugarcane liquor when a regatón comes up the river. He drinks whatever money he has, and my pots grow thinner and thinner."

"Who wants their old plastic boxes that they keep things in?" my mother asked. "Do you suppose anyone would want them?"

No one did.

"What about their coffee cups? I would take one of them. But what I really want is their tape recorder and their music. I suppose they will keep that. Probably they will keep everything good," said Teolinda.

I didn't mention the bags they slept in. I didn't think anyone else would want them. And I knew the old ladies would be upset to know that no one wanted most of their things. I knew they thought they were behaving very well by leaving us their things. But there wasn't much that we really wanted. Even the bags for sleeping. I would never sleep in the bag. Who would sleep inside a bag? But the material was soft and shiny and it would make a beautiful blouse and maybe a little dress for my daughter, whenever I had one.

☙

"Your sister and your husband are returning," my mother told me early the next morning. "They will be home soon after the old ladies leave."

"He's not my husband," I said.

My mother shrugged. She knew that the news would make me unhappy. I would be glad to see my sister, but not to see her husband, who was to be my husband too. While they were away, I could forget about her old husband. I didn't want to be married at all, and certainly not to my sister's husband. It wasn't that he was the worst man I had ever seen. But he was old. Rambi yosi. Everyone's husband is old. But if you are the younger wife, like me, then he is really old. It wasn't just that he was old either. I was happy the way I was. I didn't want to be a married woman yet. I had already lost a baby. I didn't need to have more, not yet. And if I had to be married, I wanted a husband of my own, like my

mother and like Nachi. Two women who share a husband are always competing for the things a husband
supplies—meat, firewood, the things that money buys
—cloth, beads, metal pots. Sharing the goods a husband
produces is hard. That is why co-wives fight, not because
they care who is having sex with their old husbands.
Men are careful to treat their wives equally that way—
they sleep with one one night, the other the next night.
They take one on a trip, then the other on the next trip.
But the women don't care about that. They are only
jealous of other women having sex with their boyfriends.
No one cares who her husband is having sex with.

Maya and I have always been good sisters to each
other. Even though she is older, she never bossed me
around as much as some older sisters, she never made
me do things our mother told her to do just because I
was the younger one. Maya doesn't act like an older
wife. She doesn't act like a wife at all. My mother does
all the work a wife is supposed to do, not Maya. Maya
and I had fun together; we would go off gathering
in the afternoons with our boyfriends, and I always
protected her from her husband finding out about her
boyfriends. I knew she would do the same for me, once
I had a husband.

But I was too young to be married. While they were

away, I could pretend I wasn't married. I could think I was still a young girl, not a young girl who was beginning to grow old. But now they were returning, and my whole life was going to change.

"So your old husband is coming back after all," said Elena. She sat down in my kitchen, where I was stirring a pot of deer stew. "I was beginning to think that you were not married."

"I am not married," I said. "I don't ever want to be married, never."

"Everyone is married," said Elena. "Don't be silly."

"Cuncha is not married," I said.

"Cuncha is so married."

"No, she's not. She was married, but he died."

"Yes, her *first* husband died," said Elena. "But her second husband is off working wood."

"Cuncha says he is not her husband," I said.

"Cuncha may say that, but Cuncha's father says he is her husband."

"She might as well not be married. Even if he is her husband, and I don't think he is, but even if he were, he is never here, so what difference does it make?"

Nimeran came back from hunting and brought two big birds and a live baby land turtle over to the old ladies.

"I want your boots when you leave," he said to Margarita. "They are good, strong boots. They will make it easy to hunt in the mud." Margarita took the birds, and Nimeran walked away.

Joanna came to my house later that day.

"Everyone is asking us for things. They are like vultures. I hate this."

"They are not like vultures," I said. "They are not waiting for you to die. They are waiting for you to leave. *You* said you were leaving. They just want to make sure they tell you what they want to remember you by."

Joanna laughed. "They'll remember my banana song. They'll remember my strong string. They'll remember the day of the beads. They have plenty to remember." We sat silently.

"Last night I had a dream," Joanna said. "I dreamed I was back in my apartment in New York. You were with me. We were going on a trip together. Someone came to my door. It was a delivery from a store called Macy's. They delivered a dugout canoe for our trip. We both laughed and laughed. A store in New York brought a dugout canoe to us." Joanna paused. "Isn't that a funny dream? But it was so real. So real that you and I were together in my apartment, that we would go traveling together, that we would take a trip in a canoe. So real."

Their plane was coming the next day. It would land in the river, just like the missionary planes. The old ladies had been packing the things they were taking with them. They had given a lot away. They had done it right.

That night, the night before they were going to leave, Joanna came to my house and sat down by the fire next to me.

"This is the present I want to give to you, Alicia," she said, and put something into my hand. I closed my hand around it. I knew what it was. It was her silver fish ring, the ring that her friends had given her just before she came to our village.

"I want you to have it because you have taught me many things, many, many things, and the ring is to thank you for that, and so that you will remember me when I am far away in my own country." Joanna squeezed my hand and was quiet.

"I will remember," I told her.

"I will always remember you," she said. "And Cami." She looked like she might cry. She had been crying for days, not all the time, but a lot. I did not want to sit and see her cry again.

"How could I forget a woman who calls grass vagina?" I said.

Joanna hugged me and went to her house. I put the ring on my finger. It was a beautiful ring. It looked different on me. My fingers were thinner and darker than Joanna's. The silver fish looked shinier, very beautiful.

By the next morning the old ladies had everything packed. They ate breakfast and sat on the riverbank, looking up at the sky.

"Why do they sit and look?" asked my mother. "Marco will hear the plane first, then the rest of us will hear it, and much later the old ladies will see it. Have they nothing better to do than sit and look?"

"I think they don't," I said. "I think they are sad to leave our village, happy to go back to their country, and they have no work to do, since all their pens and notebooks are packed. So they sit, hoping the plane will come soon."

"It won't come now," my mother said. "Soon it will rain."

"What? Why do you say that?" I asked her. The sky was clear and blue, no clouds at all.

"Because Joanna just took the baby land turtle down to the river and washed it."

"Why did she do that?" I muttered, and ran down to the river.

"Now your plane will not come," I told Joanna.

She looked at me. "What are you talking about? It will come. They promised to come on this day."

"But you washed the turtle," I said.

"Yes?" Joanna asked.

"So now it will rain. And those little planes do not fly when it rains. Why did you do that?"

"Because I washed the turtle it will rain?" Joanna asked.

"Of course."

"The turtle was dusty. I wanted it to be clean to take on the plane. I am giving it to our friend's son in Pucallpa. I washed it off for him. That is all. I do not want it to rain."

"Then you should not have washed the turtle," I told her

"Maybe it will not work this time," she said, drying off the turtle and walking up the riverbank. She sat next to Margarita and told her about washing the turtle.

Margarita laughed and said, "It will not rain. The

plane will come. You'll see." And they both looked up at the sky some more.

When the rains came, Joanna and Margarita went inside their house.

∾

The next morning, the old ladies were up and bathed and stirring their fire before Cuncha even arrived at their house. I went over to sit with them.

"The plane won't come this early," Cuncha told them when she got to their kitchen. She had brought them some sweet bananas for breakfast.

"We don't know when it will come," said Margarita. "And we must be ready. The plane can only come and pick us up. It cannot wait for us. The plane comes to pick us up between other jobs working for rich Americans who are looking for oil in the jungle. We must be ready when they get here, or they will leave without us."

"They would come all the way here and go all the way back without you?"

"Yes," Margarita said. "They told us so."

"Stupid old men," Cuncha muttered.

"But now that it rained on the day they were supposed to pick us up, we do not know when they will

come. They may come today, they may come tomorrow, they may come in four or five days." Joanna was
not happy. "We have to be ready."

"You should not have washed the turtle," I told her.

"If I had known it would bring rain, I would not have
washed it. I am sorry I washed it." Joanna sounded mad.
"No one told me not to wash it."

"We never told you because you never asked. Everyone here knows not to wash a turtle if you don't want
it to rain. Why would we think to tell you something
that everyone knows?" Cuncha said.

Joanna burst into tears. "I hate leaving," she said.
"And I hate it the most when you have to wait to do
it." She ran into the house and lay down.

"This is not a good way to leave," said Margarita.
"This is going to be too hard."

The old ladies waited all day. They sat in their house,
they sat in their kitchen, they sat on the riverbank.
When the sun started to set, they knew the plane would
not come that day. These little planes cannot fly at night.
After they ate, they unpacked their tape recorder and
played some of their music. Marco and I went to sit
with them. They were listening to one of their favor-

ites, some singers named after a kind of bugs. Joanna told me their name in English and what it meant in Isabo.

"Here comes my favorite line," said Joanna, who had stopped crying but now was going to start all over again. She always cried when she played her music.

"What does it say?" I asked. If she talked, she wouldn't cry.

"It says, 'In the end, at the end of it all, the love you have, the friendship you have, the love you are left with, is just the same, is only the same, as the love you gave, the love, the friendship you had for others.' "

"Of course," I said. Who didn't know that? "That is why it is so important to learn not to be stingy," I said. "Now, in the end, you finally understand."

"Yes," she said.

"But your music, your bug music, was telling you that all along."

"Yes. But the Beatles, our bug music, said it a little different. They also are saying that as much love as you have in the end is only how much love you made, how much push-push you did in your life."

"These bugs know something about life, don't they?" I said.

"Yes. They also say, 'Everybody has something to hide, except for me and my monkey.'"

We all laughed, Marco and I and Margarita and Joanna. And then we all sang together, in their English, "Everybody got something to hide 'cept for me and my monkey," and we laughed and laughed, and Marco made monkey noises, isa noises, little monkey noises that the isa monkeys make, the monkeys my people are named for, Isabo, the people of the little monkeys.

The plane did not come the next day or the next. While the old ladies waited, my mother and I tried to teach them how to pot, which they were both terrible at. Nachi tried to teach them to embroider, which Margarita was good at and Joanna awful. And Elena showed them how to weave sleeping mats. They could do that, but so slowly. Then, late one afternoon, Marco heard the plane. The old ladies were bathing in the river when Marco ran down to tell them their plane was coming. Soon we could all see the little plane flying over the treetops across the river. The old ladies got dressed very fast. They threw all the things they had unpacked back into their boxes, just as the plane came down on the river.

Joanna ran up to the pilot as he opened the door of the plane and asked him something. He laughed and nodded, and Joanna ran back to my house.

"Alicia, he says we have time to take you up in the plane, so that you can see Poincushmana from the air, the way a bird sees it. This will be our trip together. Not in a canoe but in a plane! But we have to go right now. Come, we'll go flying."

Flying! And I hadn't even asked! I ran down the riverbank and climbed into the plane with Joanna. Margarita was finishing packing. Everyone came down to see us off. Joanna was laughing and laughing. I was laughing too, but I was scared. The plane smelled awful, worse than the port in Pucallpa. I began to turn the fish ring on my finger. Joanna smiled at me, patted my hand, and showed me how to hook the belt around my waist. As soon as I did, the noise of the plane started and the plane shook and shook and then, as we were looking out the window, the river grew farther away and we could see my people on the riverbank waving. They looked smaller and smaller, and then we could see only the tops of the houses and the kitchens, lined up next to the river. And then we could see how far the jungle stretched beyond the village, and it was so big and so beautiful and our village was such a small spot compared to the enormous forest. There was a tiny canoe coming downriver. There must have been a person in it, but it was too small to tell. There, upriver, was the clearing where Cami was buried. And beyond that, mountains, big mountains, where the river rose and fell so quickly that people were drowned in an instant, up in those rapids where you could find salt. The plane turned, and now I could see the big river, with our little river flowing into it. And I could see all the little streams that fed our little river. Then we were coming down to our river again, right on top of it. The plane stopped and we were back in my old world and it looked the same as when we left it, but now I knew that it also looked different when you looked at it from another view.

I started to get out of the plane to let Margarita get in.

Joanna hugged me. I hugged her back and let go before her tears could start again.

"Era mecai. Minqui shina shina shinandai," she said. I am going now. I will think and think and think of you.

"Catanhue," I said. Go and come back.

We all stood on the riverbank and waved as the plane drove chiponqui, and then raised itself up and flew out of sight, over the treetops.

Joan Abelove lived in the Amazon jungle for two years, with people much like those portrayed in this book. She has a doctorate in cultural anthropology. She is also the author of another novel, *Saying It Out Loud*.

Joan Abelove lives in New York City with her husband and son.